WHO HOLDS THE POWER

STEPHEN TAYLOR

STEPHEN TAYLOR BOOKS

COVER DESIGN BY
DISSECT DESIGNS
WWW.DISSECTDESIGNS.COM

Copyright © 2020 Stephen Taylor
All rights reserved.
ISBN: 978-1-7391636-2-4

"All rights reserved. No part of this publication may be reproduced,
stored in a retrieval system, or transmitted in any form or by any means,
electronic, photocopying, mechanical, recording, or otherwise, without
the prior permission of the copyright owner.

All characters in this book are fictitious and any resemblance to actual
persons living or dead is purely coincidental."

DANNY PEARSON WILL RETURN

For updates about current and upcoming releases, as well as exclusive promotions, visit the authors website at:

www.stephentaylorbooks.com

ALSO BY STEPHEN TAYLOR
THE DANNY PEARSON THRILLER SERIES

To My Brother in law Steve who lost his fight with cancer as I finished this book. Rest in peace mate.

CHAPTER 1

Watching the sky, the four-strong security team shielded their eyes against the harsh sun over the Gulf of Aden. The noise grew as the silhouette of the Airbus helicopter came into view. Sand and grit stung their skin as the helicopter swung around the stern of the cargo ship before touching down gently on the helipad. Danny Pearson grabbed his rucksack and climbed out. He kept his head low as he moved away, giving a thumbs-up to the pilot when he was clear of the rotor blades. The pilot gave a thumbs-up and wound up the revs, lifting the helicopter gently off the deck before banking hard and heading back toward Assab airport, Eritrea. Danny waited for the engine noise to die down before speaking to the men.

'All right, guys. So what's so important it can't wait until you dock in Jeddah?' he said, stretching out the aches of a five-hour journey.

'Sorry, boss, we've got a bit of a situation,' said Phil, looking around to make sure they weren't overheard.

1

'Go on,' Danny said, his interest piqued.

'Last night after Matt's shift we went to the armoury to sign the weapons in and out for a shift change, as usual. I unlocked the door and found all the weapons gone. We only have the M16 and the handgun that Matt had with him and thirty rounds of ammunition.'

'Keys?' Danny asked bluntly.

'Three sets—one with me, Karl's got a set and the captain has a spare set that should be locked in his safe,' said Phil showing Danny the key.

'I assume there's more to this?'

'There's three boats a couple of miles behind us. We picked them up when we passed Berbera and they've been closing ever since,' said Matt as all five of them instinctively looked off the stern of the boat.

'Somali pirates then, with help on board? Not their usual form—they wouldn't usually take the risk,' said Danny frowning.

'You can thank the captain for that,' said Craig chipping in.

'Go on then, let's hear it,' said Danny, a bad feeling coming over him.

'Captain Targen is a dickhead of the highest order. He also likes to drink and talk way too much. We docked in Mombasa while the ship unloaded a consignment of plant machinery for some mining company. While we're in port, we come across the captain in a local bar. The stupid bastard's pissed out of his nut. Next thing we know, he's shouting his mouth off about the two million quid the mining company just paid him, in cash! Me and Matt tried to shut him up and ended up carrying him back to the ship,' said Phil as Matt nodded in agreement.

'Jesus, I bet that went round port like wildfire. Did you

2

take any new crew on at Mombasa?' asked Danny, spotting a nervous crewman watching them from behind some containers.

'Yeah, one Kenyan lad.'

'Mmm, Kenyan or Somali?' said Danny, moving to his left to take him out of the line of sight of the watching crewman.

He put a finger to his lips before sprinting away from the puzzled team, disappearing down the far side of the containers. A few seconds later they turned in unison at the sound of protests. Danny was pushing the distressed crewman towards them, twisting his arm up behind his back. Throwing him on the deck, the team stood around him while Danny started grilling him.

'What did you do with the guns?'

'I... Nothing I don't know what you're talking about,' he said nervously, shaking his head.

'Phil, shoot him and throw him over the side,' said Danny, his voice gruff and face emotionless.

Understanding Danny's intentions, Phil drew his handgun and pulled the slide to chamber a round. Without hesitation he placed the barrel on the terrified man's forehead.

'No, no, wait! I'm sorry. They made me.'

'Cut the crap and answer the question. Where's the guns?' shouted Danny, inches away from his face.

'They're gone, over the side,' he said shaking.

'You're Somali, yes?'

He nodded slowly.

'How many are coming?'

'Twelve, four in each boat.'

'What weapons have they got?' said Danny, grabbing the scared man's shirt.

'Five—I think they have five machine guns, the rest have machetes.'

'Karl, take him down and lock him in one of the storage compartments. We'll deal with him later.'

Danny stared over the bow. Shielding his eyes from the midday sun he could just make out the three boats in the distance.

'You got a spare radio?' he asked.

Phil passed him a headset. Grabbing it, he made off towards the bridge.

'Phil, you cover the port side with the M16. Matt, can you take the handgun and cover the starboard side? Gary, you rifle through the lifeboats, see if you can find any flare guns. I'm going to see the captain,' he shouted over his shoulder.

Hooking his earpiece in, Danny clanged up the metal staircase to the bridge.

'Radio check, you hear me, guys?'

'Yeah, copy that,' said Matt.

'Loud and clear. We'll get Karl back on air when he gets back above deck,' said Phil.

Danny yanked the door open and marched towards Captain Targen.

'Captain, Danny Pearson, Director of Operations for Greenwood Security. I need you to put out a distress call *now*. We are under the attack of pirates and need urgent assistance.'

The plump captain popped up out of his seat, an indignant look on his face at being interrupted on his bridge.

'Who the hell do you think you are, coming up here order—'

'Shhh! Go ahead, Phil,' said Danny holding a finger up to the red-faced captain, silencing him.

'Here they come. We've got fifteen, maybe twenty minutes.'

'Roger that, Phil,' said Danny, his face hardening and eyes boring into the captain as he turned back towards him.

'Now, you. You listen to me, you stupid bastard. If you hadn't got drunk and shouted your mouth off about the cash you've got in the safe, we wouldn't be in this mess. Now get on that fucking radio and see if any naval vessels are close by.'

With Danny still staring at him, the captain's anger turned to embarrassment. He nodded sheepishly to the radio officer to make the call.

'This is why your men are here. You're telling me you can't deal with it? What the hell do we pay you for, huh?' said the captain, finding a little attitude.

Danny noticed all the keys on the captain's desk and bit back.

'If you checked the Kenyan deckhand you took on in Mombasa was actually Kenyan and not a Somali pirate, and if you didn't leave all the fucking keys lying around instead of locking them in the safe, the bloody Somali wouldn't have got into our armoury and thrown all the weapons overboard,' shouted Danny as he threw the keys off the desk at the pompous captain.

'I...I didn't know. I'm sorry. I—'

'Zip it,' said Danny, turning to the radio operator.

'Anything?'

'Yes, sir, the aircraft carrier HMS Queen Elizabeth has responded. She's changed course and has dispatched a helicopter gunship to assist. ETA forty minutes.'

'Thanks, son. Any change, let me know over the ship's PA system.'

Danny left the bridge, leaping down the metal stairs.

'Help's coming in forty, guys,' Danny said over the headset.

'Great, they'll be here in fifteen. Any ideas what we do for the other twenty-five minutes?' said Matt.

6

CHAPTER 2

S tanding on the stern with Gary and Phil, Danny watched the boats bounce across the ship's wake as they split. Two boats went port-side while the other went starboard. Danny waved Matt and Karl over.

'Right, Phil, Gary, Matt, you keep the two boats pinned down. Stagger your rounds, boys, M16, gun, then a flare. Slowly, right? Just enough to keep their heads down until help comes, ok?' said Danny, waving them off and turning to Karl.

'Ok, we'll try to keep the boat on the starboard side busy. Take a scout around, find anything that we can throw at these guys,' said Danny, just as erratic automatic fire pinged in all directions off the containers above them.

Staying low they moved starboard, keeping the blue ragged fishing boat in their sights as it bounced around in the waves from the ship, working its way down the side of the boat. Two skinny black Somalis struggled on the deck with an aluminium ladder, hooks tied to the top. They fought against the bouncing swell, scraping it along the side of the ship in an effort to hook it over the deck rail.

7

Karl appeared next to Danny with fire extinguishers from below deck and a heavy hook from the ship's cargo crane. He dropped them and headed off to find more ammunition.

Seeing the ladder find its hold on the rail, Danny ran to the edge and hurled the fire extinguishers down at the pirates below. They found a target, striking one of the men on his shoulder as he came up the ladder. He crashed to the deck, screaming in pain and surprise.

Seeing the pirate by the wheelhouse swing his rifle up, Danny hit the deck as a hail of bullets ricocheted around him. He heard a cry from behind him and turned to see Karl on the floor holding his leg, a bullet wound bleeding from his thigh. Grabbing the hook, Danny hurled it down at the gunman. It narrowly missed him, clanging off the roof of the wheelhouse. Ducking back out of the line of sight, Danny grabbed Karl under the armpits and dragged him out of harm's way between the containers. Behind them the furious Somali pirate let rip with wild blasts of gunfire.

'Keep the pressure on,' said Danny, taking his jacket off and wrapping it around the wound.

'I'm fine, boss, go, go,' said Karl through gritted teeth.

Leaving him, Danny climbed up on top of the two-storey containers. Gunfire echoed out from the other side of the boat.

'Phil, Gary, you ok, guys?'

'Yeah, we just threw the ladder back at them. They went nuts but I think we can keep them pinned down,' said Phil over more gunfire.

'Ok, keep it up,' said Danny as he hopped across from container to container. He ended up directly above two pirates as they clambered over the railings. Both men had Kalashnikov rifles hanging across their shoulders. One of

8

them looked along the deck while the other waved and shouted down to the injured man on the fishing boat.

Crouching on the edge of the container, Danny dropped from above. He grabbed the skinny Somali from behind and planted a boot firmly on the back of the other pirate as he shouted down the ladder, the blow knocking him clean over the railings. Screaming as he fell, the pirate crashed through the roof of the wheelhouse and landed on top of the skipper, knocking him out. The boat veered away from the ship, leaving a man stranded on the ladder.

Back on deck, Danny punched the gunman several times in the head, putting him out cold. Stepping away, the hairs stood up on the back of his neck.

He sensed someone coming at him from behind.

Danny threw himself to one side as a razor-sharp machete tore through his T-shirt. The skinny Somali came at him again, swinging the long blade.

Danny backed along the deck, avoiding the slices of the machete.

A burst of gunfire echoed from the other side of the ship, making the Somali man look through the gap in the containers. Danny flew forwards, pushing the machete aside and powering a punch to the man's throat. He fell to the floor, dropping the blade, coughing and gasping for air. Picking it up, Danny threw the machete overboard and kicked the man in the balls for good measure. Leaving him in a heap, he picked up the Kalashnikov and went to help on the other side of the ship.

Running across the deck, the low *whomp* of helicopter rotor blades stopped him as the naval gunship boomed overhead. It banked to one side, the deafening sound of large-calibre gunfire sent white-hot tracers across the sky, warning the Somali pirates off. Turning hard through the ship's wake, the little boats nearly capsized as they headed back towards Berbera as fast as they could.

The gunship circled around a couple more times before touching down on the helipad. Eight marines jumped out onto the deck as Phil, Matt and Gary went to greet them.

'Man, are we glad to see you guys,' said Phil, shaking the officer in charges hand.

Before the marine could respond, Danny came round the corner with Karl's arm around his neck as he hopped towards them.

'Have you guys got a medic on board?'

'Yes, sir. MEDIC!' the marine shouted.

Two men rushed to Danny and helped Karl off him.

'Thanks. You might want to check out the two Somali pirates on the starboard deck while you're at it,' said Danny, hearing his sat phone ringing. It was his friend and owner of Greenwood Security, Paul Greenwood. Looking around at his team, the medics, and the marines marching the Somali pirates around the deck, he answered.

'Eh, hi, Paul.'

'Would anyone like to explain why I've had Rear Admiral Hector Crane on the phone? About a major incident in international waters involving you and a scrambled helicopter gunship with eight marines on board,' said Paul, less than impressed.

'Eh, well, it's like this, Paul...'

CHAPTER 3

Walking through the south gate, Lee Crossman entered Kowloon Park in the Tsim Sha Tsui region of Hong Kong. Moving up the steps, he headed through the lush greenery towards the park's lotus pond. He checked his watch as he passed the lake with its flock of pink flamingos, pleased that he was still five minutes early. Spotting the bench he'd been told to meet at, he sat down and checked his watch again and waited. Lee looked around for his contact and struggled to keep his excitement under wraps. If the information from this guy checked out, it would be the story of a lifetime. A scoop like this was a freelance journalist's dream. Get it right and he could write his own ticket. Concentrating on the present, Lee spotted a nervous-looking Chinese man hurrying in his direction. He looked behind himself several times as he approached.

'Mr Crossman?'

'Please call me Lee. It's Jian, yes?'

'Yes,' he said looking around again.

'Have you got the information, Jian?' said Lee, trying to get him to focus.

'Yes, you can get the money?' said Jian, pulling a book-sized Jiffy bag out of his pocket. He held it close to him, staring intently at Lee, waiting for confirmation.

'If this is what you say it is, I'll have people queueing up to pay for it.'

Jian relaxed a little and gave Lee the Jiffy bag, his hand shaking a little as he did so.

'It is. I was Cheng Haku's personal assistant for five years. I saw him with your man several times. This information is from Haku's personal computer. It's all in there —the money, your man and an American, and the man they had killed.'

Jian looked at his watch.

'I have to go. Call me on my cell when you have the mon—'

Jian froze in mid-sentence, his eyes wide in terrified surprise. His lips moved in silent conversation before he coughed. A dribble of thick red blood oozed out of his mouth, soaking into his white shirt. He slumped onto the bench, dead.

Lee jumped up, shocked. The ancient ivory carved-dragon handle of a throwing knife was impaled to the hilt between Jian's shoulder blades. Panicking, Lee looked up and down the path. A Chinaman stood stock-still in a crisp black suit, staring intensely. He started to move forward, then stopped as a group of tourists moved up the path. They were too busy taking pictures of the flamingos and selfies to take much notice of him. His face was expressionless and his eyes dark and narrow and cold as they bore into Lee.

Oh, Christ. Shit, I've gotta get out of here.

Fear and adrenaline kicking him into action, Lee was

up, hurrying around the lake. He weaved through a group of school kids on a day trip, before running down the path. Risking a glance behind him, his heart pounded in his chest as he saw the Chinaman following nimbly—almost gliding—through the school party.

Lee turned and ran. Screams echoed from the lotus pond as tourists came across Sheng's body. Leaving the park by a different exit, Lee crossed the road and entered the China Hong Kong City shopping mall. With his mind racing and heart pounding, he weaved through the crowds of shoppers before tucking into a shop doorway. He peeped between the sales displays and looked back at the mall entrance.

The Chinaman moved through the entrance. He walked a few paces then stood intently still. As shoppers moved around him, the plain-suited Chinaman failed to register in their consciousness as they went about their day. His cold eyes searched faces, slowly, logically, from left to right and then back again.

Lee stooped down low and moved out, slipping through the shoppers as he went deeper into the shopping mall. Passing a post office, Lee stopped. He moved inside and nervously joined the queue, peering behind him every few seconds until he got to the counter. Taking a pen out of his pocket, he wrote an address on the Jiffy bag. Rummaging through his pockets, Lee found a piece of paper and wrote a message on it before sealing it in the Jiffy bag. With his hands shaking as he paid the woman on the counter for registered air mail, Lee tucked the proof of postage in his wallet and left. He poked his head out of the post office door and tentatively checked both ways.

He couldn't see the Chinaman anywhere.

Fighting the urge to run, Lee walked as fast as he could out of the shopping mall. His heart pounded as he continued along Canton Road to the Star Ferry terminal by the clock tower. With a sigh of relief, he bought a ticket to Hong Kong Island and boarded a ferry just as it was preparing to leave. He climbed the stairs and went out onto the open deck at the rear of the boat. Still jumpy he sat down on a bench on his own; there was only a handful of passengers on the deck and they were mostly around the railings, watching as the boat moved away from the ferry terminal.

Calming himself down, Lee watched the terminal as it grew smaller. Just putting some distance from Tsim Sha Tsui and the chilling image of the Chinaman helped him collect his thoughts. He fetched his phone out of his pocket and made a call.

Shit, answerphone.

'Kate, it's Lee. Listen, I've stumbled onto something big in Hong Kong. My contact's been killed and I think I'm in danger. I've sent you a package, sis. It's incredibly important so keep it safe for me, ok? I'll be on the next available flight out of here, ok? See you soon.'

He hung up and sat back, working out his next move.

Get back to the hotel, pack, and book the first flight out of here.

A toot on the ship's horn made him look up when they were halfway across the bay; the ferry from the island was passing them on its way back to Tsim Sha Tsui. Lee smiled at a couple of kids waving across at it, their mothers paying no attention as they talked to each other. He felt a prick on his neck like a mosquito bite and instinctively went to raise his hand to rub it. He looked down in confusion when it didn't move. A rush of panic hit him as he tried and failed to move his other hand.

Oh god, I can't move.

Out of the corner of his eye, he saw the Chinaman walk casually around the bench and sit down beside him.

14

He reached over and pulled a tiny dart out of Lee's neck, tucking it into an ornate wrist band hidden under the sleeve of his suit.

'The neurotoxin from a Columbian golden frog. The smallest amount will paralyse a man before shutting all the body functions down. Do not worry, you won't feel any pain. Now, you have something that belongs to my client.'

While Lee screamed silently in his head, the Chinaman went through his pockets. When he couldn't find the Jiffy bag he frowned and turned his attention to Lee's wallet. Locked in his personal nightmare, Lee lost control of his diaphragm and his breathing stopped. Tears dropped from his unblinking eyes as he felt his heartbeat slow to a halt. In the last seconds before endless darkness took him, the boat turned and backed into its mooring. Unable to move his eyes, Lee stared at Hong Kong Island until it faded out of consciousness. The Chinaman pulled the post office receipt from Lee's wallet; he smiled at the time, date and delivery address printed on it. Tucking it into his pocket, he got up and strolled off the boat. An unremarkable man in an ordinary suit, invisible in plain sight as he disembarked with all the other passengers.

CHAPTER 4

'Ladies and gentlemen, please give a warm welcome to a very special guest speaker to this year's green energy seminar: Mr Cheng Haku, founder of Haku Industries.'

The host stepped back from the podium and shook hands with Haku as he took his place.

'Good evening, ladies and gentlemen. Thank you for inviting me to this prestigious and globally important event. We all know the urgency with which we need to implement clean, environmentally-friendly, green energy solutions to the planet. In my home country alone, we have over 500 coal-fired power stations and 45 nuclear power stations. For two decades, we at Haku Industries have been working on the development of hydrogen energy to power our planet. As you know, it is in abundant supply and has a zero-carbon footprint with a by-product of $H2O$. The main problem has always been the large-scale manufacture of hydrogen; stripping it from gasses such as methane, natural gas or fossil fuels has been the most effective method in the past. But this still leaves us dependent on the earth's resources we are trying to avoid. I am proud to announce that Haku Industries has perfected a method of extracting hydrogen from saltwater, with the by-product of clean, safe drinking water.'

Haku paused while rapturous applause filled the room. When it died down he continued.

'Thank you, thank you. Our flagship hydrogen power station in Macau can generate enough power for a city the size of Hong Kong and also supply them with eighty percent of their drinking water. In light of these results, Haku Industries is in talks with the United Kingdom and the USA to replace all their coal-fired power stations over the next twenty years. My esteemed members of the European Community, I wish to bring this technology beyond the U.K. and U.S.A. I want to power the world, cleanly, safely, and provide drinking water to countries that suffer drought and famine,' said Haku, enjoying the adoration as the room clapped and cheered in a standing ovation.

Haku smiled and waved as he walked off the stage and headed down the back corridor towards his courtesy room. The smile reserved for the crowd was long gone from his face as he scowled at his phone. His bodyguard followed him a few steps back with an expression of disinterest on his face.

'I don't wish to be disturbed,' Haku said bluntly before slamming the door on the bodyguard.

Alone, he made the call.

'I've been waiting. Why haven't I heard from you?' he said impatiently down the phone.

'There has been a complication. Our friend met with a journalist and gave him the item in question. Both parties have been silenced, but the journalist mailed the package to an address in Vienna before I could get to

17

him,' said the Chinaman in a monotone voice with no hint of emotion.

'What?! If that information gets out, we're all finished. Get it back!' Haku yelled, his head spinning with the consequences of his failure.

'The chairman is aware of the situation, Mr Haku. I am on my way to Austria, the matter will be resolved shortly. In future I would advise you to hold your tongue when you speak to me,' continued the Chinaman with a chilling assertiveness to the last sentence.

Haku quickly put his anger in check, a little fear taking its place.

'Of course, I'm sorry, I meant no disrespect. I look forward to the matter being res—' said Haku tailing off. The Chinaman had already hung up on him.

He sat back in the chair, his hands shaking a little. Taking a few deep breaths, he stood and opened the door. With the mask of arrogance back on his face, he clicked his fingers at the bodyguard.

'You, get them to bring the car around, we are leaving.'

'Yes, Mr Haku, at once, sir,' he said, turning away to talk into his radio.

CHAPTER 5

After both his flights were delayed, Danny finally entered Heathrow Terminal 3 Arrivals. He was tired, hungry and fed up. It had taken several days of reports, interviews and meetings with the client to clear up the cargo ship incident, and he was glad to be home. He grabbed a sandwich and a coffee. Flicking his phone off airplane mode he ripped the cellophane lid off his BLT, devouring the sandwich at record speed. As the signal kicked in, messages beeped their arrival while he washed the sandwich down with hot coffee. Danny scrolled down and smiled.

Oi, Captain Birdseye. Are you back from playing with your toy boats?

I've got a case of beer and a take-out with your name on it. Scott.

. . . .

A little more refreshed, Danny hooked his backpack over his shoulder and left the arrivals hall, making for the taxi rank. Ahead of him in the pickup bay, the chauffeur of a large black limousine walked around the car and opened the back door. He stood upright and, without saying a word, gestured inside. Even though Danny wasn't particularly worried, his muscles tensed; he was ready to take out the driver and move if he had to. He glanced inside the car.

'Mr Pearson, be a good chap and get in,' said Howard, looking exactly as Danny had last seen him, with his expensive Savile Row suit and neatly cut hair.

Fighting the urge to walk away, he got in. He owed the agency man for his help with the Russian Mafia a few years back, it was a debt he couldn't ignore. The chauffeur shut the door and moved back round to the driver's seat; he glanced in the rear-view mirror as he pulled slowly into traffic.

'Take the scenic route please, Gerald, and could we have some privacy please?' said Howard, his tone upbeat.

'Certainly, sir.'

The driver flicked a switch and a glass divide slid up between the passenger and driver's compartments.

'It's good to see you, Daniel. You look well.'

'Cut the crap, Howard, what do you want?' said Danny, barely hiding his annoyance.

'To the point as always. I'll dispense with the niceties then. I have something I need you to do for me.'

'Go on.'

'I need you to go to Vienna, pick up a package for me and bring it back,' said Howard in the same way he'd ask someone to pop down the shop and get him some milk.

'What kind of package?' said Danny suspiciously.

'Not sure, old boy, hard drive or a memory stick

perhaps. Might even be a notebook. All we know is that it contains information.'

'Why don't you get one of your goons to do it? What's the catch, Howard?' said Danny, his patience wearing thin.

'There is a problem in the department and until that problem is identified, I would rather use, erm, acquaintances, shall we say, outside the department.'

'Ok, tell me about the package. Who has it and who's after it?' Danny said, sitting back in his seat. It was nice to have the boot on the other foot—Howard needed him, so he could push for more information.

'Mm, ok. In brief, we were set to do an exchange in Hong Kong for some information regarding our problem. Our man has disappeared, and a journalist called Lee Crossman got wind of the story and offered the contact a deal. Now the contact is dead, Lee Crossman is dead, and our man turned up in a back alley with an antique Chinese dagger pushed through his ear into his brain. That was yesterday. At 5 a.m. today, Lee Crossman's sister walks into a Vienna police station, concerned about a message on her phone left by her brother, something about a murder, being in danger, and a package he says he's sent her. The police sent her away as (1) she hasn't got the package yet, and (2) her brother was murdered in Hong Kong so there's nothing they can do. Our best guess is the package will arrive sometime in the next twenty-four hours, which is probably the same amount of time it will take for the Hong Kong authorities to inform her that her brother is dead,' said Howard handing Danny small file.

Danny opened it to find a photo of Kate with her address and a bundle of Austrian euros.

'And what about the woman?' said Danny looking Howard straight in the eye.

'What about her? Tell her you're sorry for her loss?

Give her the euros, use your initiative, or you could use the fake Interpol ID in there and tell her you're investigating her brother's death,' said Howard with a smug smile.

Danny looked into the file and fished the ID out to see his photo on it.

'Any idea who killed the men in Hong Kong?'

'Nothing concrete. There are rumours of a contractor called the Chinaman. Likes to use ancient Chinese weapons and leaves no trace, in and out like a ghost.'

Howard pressed the intercom to the driver.

'Take us back please, Gerald,' he said. Reaching inside his suit jacket he pulled out an airline ticket and handed it to Danny.

'Your flight leaves in the morning. I'll see you when you get back.'

'How do I get hold of you?' said Danny looking at the ticket.

'There's a card in there, just call and ask for an appointment. I'll get back to you.'

Danny found the business card and read it.

'Oxford Financial Consultants.'

No address, just a number under the name.

The chauffeur pulled up where they'd begun; he got out and opened the door for Danny. He got out and walked to the taxi rank, watching the large black limousine slide past him and disappear out of sight.

I've got a bad feeling about this.

CHAPTER 6

The sun was setting below the rooftops by the time the taxi pulled up outside Danny's three-bed terraced house in Walthamstow. He paid the taxi driver and threw open the front door, clicking the lights on as he kicked the door shut behind him. The house felt cold and empty as he walked into the kitchen. Trisha had broken up with him a couple of months ago and he'd hardly been back since. The house was showing obvious signs of the break-up; gaps in the cupboards and items vanished from the worktops and shelves echoed her absence. He felt a sadness inside but didn't blame her. Danny had an intensity and wildness about him that some women found attractive. The trouble was that the same thing that attracted them was the thing that ended up infuriating them and driving them away. The only woman that ever really got him was his late wife, Sarah. She and their son, Timothy, had been killed some years ago. Crushed in their car by a lorry driven by revengeful psychopath Nicholas Snipe, the loss had destroyed Danny and caused him to leave the SAS. Shaking memories away to return to the now, Danny slung his rucksack down, grabbed his phone and text a message back to his oldest friend, Scott.

Sorry, you old tart, you'll have to put the beers back in the fridge.

I've got to get a flight early in the morning, someone called a favour in.

Should only be two or three days. I'll call you when I'm back.

A message came back seconds after Danny had pressed send.

I'd rather not know, old boy. Last time you did a favour
for someone, I nearly got killed.

Danny chuckled and thumbed a slow reply.

I was doing the favour for you, you posh prick.

Again, the reply pinged barely a moment after he'd sent it.

Now, now, you caveman. Don't think too hard, you'll give
yourself a headache. See you when you get back.

Danny smiled again.

24

How does he type so bloody fast?

He went upstairs to shower and freshen up. The bedroom seemed empty and depressing. The wardrobe rattled with empty hangers, and he missed Trisha's bits and bobs in the bathroom that used to drive him nuts.

Fuck it.

He dressed and went out the front door, climbing into his dusty, unused BMW M4. It started up with a reassuring growl and made him smile as he headed off with a throaty rasp. After only ten minutes he pulled up outside the old Georgian four-bedroom semi he'd grown up in. After their mother died, Danny insisted his brother Rob had the house. During the years Danny had been fighting overseas, Rob had nursed their mother through her battle with cancer until it finally got the better of her. He felt his brother had earned it. After ringing the bell, he watched the skinny shadow approaching the stained glass of the front door. When Rob opened it, his face lit up to see him.

'Evening, you going to let me in then, Titch?'

'Yeah, come in, stranger, I wondered when you'd turn up,' said Rob smiling, happy to see his brother.

Danny followed Rob into the kitchen, which despite being changed many times, remained the heart of the home and had been since Danny and Rob sat with their parents as kids.

'Danny, good to see you back,' said Tina, rushing around the kitchen table to hug him.

'Hiya, Tina, good to be back, if only briefly,' said Danny shrugging.

'Oh, sounds ominous. Where are you off to?'

'Just a quick trip to Vienna tomorrow. Should be back by the weekend.'

'Beer, brov?' said Rob, fishing some cans out of the fridge.

25

'Yes please, Rob, that would just hit the spot, mate,' he said, catching the can as Rob tossed it.

'You want some dinner? I've cooked a curry—there's plenty to go around,' said Tina, returning to a big pot on the cooker.

'You just said the magic words, Tina.'

CHAPTER 7

Wesley and Andrew Mason waited in the boardroom, looking out the floor-to-ceiling-glass window at the modern expanse of buildings across Silicon Valley, California. The brothers had been snapped up by ECB Power after leaving MIT; they were at the end of a four-year project for the R&D department. The product was ecologically-sound battery-cell technology, half the size and twice the power of the best lithium-ion battery. With a battery section under the boot of a family saloon, it could power a car for 600 miles and fully recharge in 15 minutes. They turned their attention back to the room as the door opened and company CEO Ian McClusky walked in.

'Congratulations, gentlemen, let me shake your hand,' he said marching over to them. Ian smiled warmly as he shook their hands and patted them on the back.

'Thank you,' they both said in unison.

'I've got to tell you, the board is ecstatic. The chairman wants to start mass production through our factory in Germany immediately. He wants the product in at least three of the major car manufacturers by Christmas,' said Ian, standing back with his arms wide in a celebratory gesture.

'Er, wow. That's amazing, Mr McClusky, but we have another six months' product testing to do,' said Wesley while Andrew nodded in agreement.

'Look, boys, the product works. Yes? The board won't wait, they have contracts with the car giants. This thing's huge, and talking of huge, I've got your bonuses here,' he said, taking two envelopes out of his pocket.

'Thanks, but I still think we should run more tests,' said Andrew more forcefully.

'Look, guys, just take your bonuses and move onto the next project. Don't make waves, ok? What the chairman wants, the chairman gets.'

The brothers finally took the hint and left the room. Ian sat on the corner of the desk, dabbing the sweat off his forehead. He pulled a bottle of antacids out of his pocket and shook some into his mouth. His stomach was burning with the stress of the past five years. The pressure as a board member to deliver had been exhausting, and the funding to get there had been enormous. Even after five years Ian had never personally met the chairman. All communication went through secure email communication and the chairman's encrypted video conferencing system. What was more worrying was the chairman's plans for world reform; talk of payoffs in Africa and board members in key positions in the Kremlin and Beijing.

Ian's stomach kicked off again as he thought about Rami Patel and Hanz Truman, two board members who aired their disapproval of the chairman's proposals. Within a week all trace of them had gone. Their disappearance spoke volumes.

No one had challenged the chairman's plans since then.

CHAPTER 8

Exiting passport control into the arrivals hall at Vienna International Airport, Danny headed towards the exit. He wasn't sure if he was just tired from two days of plane travel and airports, or if the airport police were actually paying him more attention than they should be. Without looking over, he caught glances his way on the edge of his peripheral vision. The following radio chat confirmed it: they had been waiting for his arrival. But why? He carried on walking, expecting to be pulled up at any minute. When he got through the exit to the taxi rank without approach, he started to think he was overtired and imagining it. He gave the address he had for Kate Crossman, in the Landstrasse region of Vienna, and sat back, watching out the window as the architecture grew grander and more flamboyant the closer they got to Vienna's centre.

The driver pulled up outside an 18th century five-storey apartment block. Danny paid the driver and went over to the communal entrance door. Before he could press the buzzer, he noticed the forced lock. The door was slightly ajar. The hairs on the back of his neck stood on end.

Sliding silently into the foyer, Danny avoided the lift and headed up the stairs three steps at a time. He stopped short of the door to the fourth floor and caught his breath. Looking through the small square window in the door he checked out the corridor in both directions.

All quiet.

He made his way along the corridor, treading lightly. He clocked the split door jamb on the lock side of apartment 23 as he approached. Danny stood to one side and placed his hand on the door. He pushed it open an inch and stopped, listening. He could hear scrapes of furniture being moved, followed by a woman swearing. Relieved, he pushed the door open and poked his head inside.

'Hello, Miss Crossman. Are you ok?'

'No, I'm bloody not and who the hell are you?' she said, putting her coffee table upright in the trashed apartment.

'Eh, Trevor White, Interpol. I'm sorry but it's not safe for you here,' said Danny doing his best to sound official.

'It's ok, I've just called the police, they're sending someone over,' she said, eyeing him up and down with a frown.

'Miss Crossman, I think the police might be part of the problem. Look, it's not safe here. Your brother sent you something? There are people out there prepared to kill for it. Have you still got it?'

'How do I know I can trust you?' she said, her eyes wide and scared as she backed away towards a block of kitchen knives.

'If you couldn't you'd be dead by now. Do you have it?' Danny said forcefully. This was taking too long.

'Yes, it's in my bag. I went out to clear my head and

found this mess when I returned,' she said, still looking uneasily at him.

'Ok, grab your bag, money and passport and come with me. We can go anywhere, your choice, a bar, or a coffeehouse, somewhere public if you like, anywhere but here. Ok?'

She looked at him for a while, thinking about what he said. She decided to trust him, suddenly moving around the apartment, grabbing her bag and shoving her purse and passport in it. Danny turned and checked the corridor was clear before walking out with Kate behind him. Reaching the door to the stairs, he turned to check Kate was following. She was a little way back putting her jacket on and zipping it up. The ding of the lift arriving sounded as she passed it.

Shit, no, no, no.

An arm shot out through the open lift door, grabbed Kate's ponytail and dragged her into the lift. Danny dropped his backpack and bolted back to the lift, just managing to duck to one side as the Chinaman threw a razor-sharp throwing star from inside. It embedded itself into the wall besides Danny's ear. He tried to get forward as the lift doors shut, only managing to watch as the image of the Chinaman with one arm around Kate's neck disappeared.

With anger and adrenaline pumping through his body, Danny powered through the door to the stairs, scooping up his backpack as he went. He jumped down the steps a flight at a time. Bursting out onto the second-floor corridor, he thumped the lift call button. With his backpack in front of him, he placed his foot on the wall opposite and launched himself through the lift doors as they pinged open.

The Chinaman was prone for action with a three-pronged dagger in each hand, one at Kate's neck pinning her in the corner, and the other forward to the lift doors.

The ferocity of Danny's attack caught him off guard. The daggers sunk into the backpack as Danny headbutted him over the top of it. The blow sent the Chinaman thumping into the back of the lift. Danny grabbed Kate's arm and jumped up. Planting both feet into the Chinaman's chest, he kicked out as hard as he could. The released energy propelled both him and Kate out of the lift as the doors slid shut. Just before they closed completely Danny saw the Chinaman pop upright, no expression on his face, but his eyes burned furiously as they stared back at him. Picking himself up, Danny grabbed Kate as she shook.

'Are you ok?' he said, trying to gain eye contact.

She took a second or two to pull herself together before nodding at him.

'Good. Kate, is there another way out of the building?'

'Eh, there's a metal fire escape that runs down the rear.'

Without replying, Danny led her along the corridor, knocking on apartment doors as they went. When the third one opened, he grabbed Kate's hand and barged past the little old lady that answered. She shrieked and yelled at him in Austrian as he hurried to the lounge window. Opening it, he climbed onto the metal fire escape. Pulling Kate along with him, he ran half-pulling her to the ground floor.

The courtyard at the bottom had an alley exiting to the street; it served as a fire escape to Kate's building and the apartment buildings behind it. Ignoring the alley, Danny went for the other apartment building. He charged the fire exit door, kicking the lock with a powerful blow. The door blew inwards with splinters of the frame and lock clanging down the corridor. Kate followed him as he made for the front entrance. Danny glanced both ways.

No Chinaman, no police.

He put his arm around Kate and walked casually out the building, like any normal couple strolling out of their apartment block. He flagged down the first taxi they saw and asked for the city centre.

———

Up on the fire escape outside Kate's fourth-floor apartment, the Chinaman stood motionless. He watched as Danny kicked the door in and disappeared. Taking a handkerchief out of his lapel pocket he dabbed the cut on his head. Tucking it neatly back into his pocket, he turned and disappeared back into the apartment.

CHAPTER 9

The taxi ride was silent and awkward. The driver dropped them off in the centre of Vienna by the Hofburg Imperial Palace. Kate followed Danny numbly, her thoughts lost in confusion and shock. They walked along Heldenplatz and ducked into the first cafe they came across. Danny ignored the waiter as he pulled the chair out on the table by the window, preferring to take one at the back with a wall behind him and a full view of the window and the door in front. Kate sat beside him, pale and shaking slightly.

'It's ok, we're safe here,' Danny said, putting his hand on her shoulder to reassure her.

'Why is this happening and what's happened to my brother?'

'Your brother's dead, sorry. They killed him in Hong Kong two days ago.'

Kate looked up at him, tears building in her eyes.

'Because of the package. What is it?' she asked, pulling it and a tissue out of her bag.

'I don't know. I was just sent here to get it,' he said, calling the waiter over.

He ordered two coffees while Kate pulled herself together.

'Sorry, who did you say you were again? Trevor something from Interpol?'

Danny could tell by the look she gave him, she was rationalising the situation. A strange man shows up, another stranger man tries to kill her, and her brother's dead. A lot to take in, in the space of an hour.

'I'm going level with you. My name is Danny Pearson. I work for British intelligence and they sent me here to get that package, that's all I know. When I arrived at the airport the police were watching me. It was probably them who turned your apartment over. The Chinaman in the lift is a contract killer, it's likely he killed your brother and the guy who gave him the package, as well as a British agent in Hong Kong. Whatever's in that package, it's important enough to kill for, and whoever wants it is connected enough to get the police involved to get it back.'

'What am I supposed to do?' she said, more together now.

'Let me make a call. I'll work something out, ok?' Danny said, trying to reassure her. She nodded slowly as the waiter brought the drinks.

'I'll just be outside, ok? You can see me through the window.'

'Ok,' she said quietly.

Outside the cafe, he called Paul.

———

Paul Greenwood was having lunch with Howard at Simpson's restaurant in The Savoy Hotel off the Strand.

They sat in a Victorian-styled oak-panelled room with red leather chairs. The conversation paused as the waiter served the wine. Their eyes followed him off before it continued again.

'You were saying,' said Paul.

'Person or persons unknown are working against us in Whitehall. Missions have been compromised and operatives have been lost,' said Howard in between mouthfuls of succulent steak.

'Any idea who they are?'

'Rumors only, I'm afraid. The mysterious Chinaman keeps coming up, and a group called 'the board'. I have my eye on the foreign minister, Lord Ravenmere. He's incredibly rich, with investments in green energy companies throughout America, Germany and China. Not strange in itself, but a certain American senator friend of his has been stirring the pot in the Middle East: Iran, Arab Emirates, Saudi. If the USA went to war in the Middle East and we followed, I would imagine a group at the forefront of green energy would do extremely well out of any instability in the oil states, don't you think?' Howard said, raising his eyebrows and his drink.

Paul was about to answer when his mobile rang.

'Danny.'

'Paul, I need to talk to Howard. The shit's hit the fan.'

'I'm with him now, what's happened?'

'The Chinaman's here, he tried to kill Kate Crossman and I think the local police were waiting for me as I came into the country.'

'Has he got the package?' said Howard over the table.

'Yes, tell Howard I've got it,' said Danny hearing him in the background.

Paul nodded to Howard and continued to talk to

Danny as the hotel concierge brought a beautifully carved mahogany box to the table.

'Get out of Austria, Danny. But don't fly. If the police are in on it, they'll pick you up straight away. Take a train or coach, quickest route out—Czech Republic perhaps—then fly home from there,' said Paul as Howard spoke to the maître d'.

'What's this, Nigel?'

'A courier just dropped it off for you, sir.'

'Did he say anything?' said Howard, puzzled.

'He just said it was a gift for the two gentlemen at this table,' said Nigel, looking at the ornate dragons carved in the lid.

Howard put his hands either side of the box. It was about the size of a shoe box.

'Let's have a look what's inside, shall we?' he said, moving to open it.

At the same time, Paul glanced out the window as he talked to Danny. He froze at what he saw.

'It can't be him, he's in... Howard, don't open that b—'

The explosion ripped through the restaurant, blowing the windows out in a boom that shook the whole building. The Chinaman watched without flinching. Satisfied, he turned and strolled off through the screams and cries of the bystanders on the busy street.

CHAPTER 10

P aul, Paul!' shouted Danny, but the line was dead. He kept his back to the window while he tried to think. He didn't want Kate to see the concern on his face. He dialled another number and waited for an answer.

'Hi, this is Scott Miller Software Inc. I'm unavailable at present. Please leave your name and number and I'll get back to you.'

'Hi, Scott, it's Danny. I need your help, mate. I think something's happened to Paul. Can you see what you can find out? Let me know on this number. Thanks, buddy.'

Hiding his frustration Danny went back inside. Howard's words echoed in his head: *Just get the information*, but seeing Kate sitting lost and alone he knew he couldn't just leave her in danger.

'Is there anyone in Vienna they might try and use against you? Family, boyfriend, anyone?' he said trying not to alarm her again.

She looked at him shocked before answering.

'Eh. No, the apartment was our parents', I'm only over here to check on it and have a week's holiday.'

'Good, because we have to get out of Austria,' said Danny looking her in the eyes, happy to see she was taking it in.

Different people deal with life and death experiences in different ways; some freak out, some just go into a bubble, blocking the world out, and some are made of tougher stuff and just get on with it. He was glad to see Kate was made of tougher stuff.

'After today that suits me fine, I'm happy to get on a plane back to London ASAP,' she said managing a smile.

'Sorry, Kate, if the police are in on this, we'll never get past the airport terminal. We should take a train to the Czech Republic, then fly out from there.'

'Prague, there's a big airport in Prague. I got diverted there once, an engine failure—don't ask. It's about a three-and-a-half-hour train journey. You have to get the train from the station at Vienna Airport,' she said looking more relaxed as she finished her coffee.

Danny opened his backpack up and pulled out a hoody and passed it to Kate.

'Here, put this on, put the hood up when we go for the train.'

She nodded and pulled it over her head. Danny looked at the two sets of holes that pierced the front where the Chinaman's three-pronged daggers had been.

'Hmm, not the greatest look but it will have to do,' said Danny with a smile.

Kate looked down and put her fingers through the holes.

'Thank you,' she whispered.

'What for?'

'Being there, saving my life.'

The emotion caught him off guard, so he just gave a nod and a simple, 'That's ok.'

He delved into his backpack again, mostly to avoid the awkward silence, and brought out his favourite baseball cap. He checked it for holes and grinned when he found none.

'Ok, now we're ready,' he said.

CHAPTER 11

Good afternoon, Mr Chairman, or should I say good morning where you are?'

'Good afternoon will do just fine, Lord Ravenmere. I assume you're calling to confirm the removal of our interfering friend,' the chairman said looking at Lord Hubert Ravenmere on a screen in the wall of screens across one end of the boardroom.

'Yes, I'm glad to say that situation is now resolved.'

'Let's not get ahead of ourselves, there is still the matter of Haku's carelessness and the item that still needs to be recovered in Vienna,' the chairman said coldly.

'Relax, I've spoken to Gustav. He's flagged the man and the women as wanted terrorists, his officers have Vienna locked down, the airport, train and bus stations are all being watched and there are roadblocks out of the city.'

'Relax, really, Hubert. Do I need to remind you we have no idea what information is on that hard drive? If the content is made public, it could be the end of all of us,' said the chairman to an uneasy silence.

'No, no, you don't,' Hubert said with rather less bravado.

'What do you know about the man Howard sent?'

'Very little I'm afraid, he's not one of the usual assets. My best guess is Howard recruited him, off grid.'

'Mmm, the Chinaman says he's good, whoever he is. Let me know the second you have the situation under control.'

The chairman turned the video call off before Hubert had time to answer. He sat back in deep thought for a while before tapping on the keyboard in front of him. A screen in the centre of the wall burst into life with the image of a middle-aged man, his features hard and weathered under his military buzz-cut.

'General, how was your meeting with the president?'

'Very good, Mr Chairman. The growing tension in Iran and the breakdown in communications with the Saudi Arabia has prompted the council to seek my advice on a war plan,' the general said with the calm assertiveness you'd expect from a man of his position.

'Excellent, General, and our plans to escalate the situation?'

'The plans are in place to take out the American Embassy in Baghdad, we have the assets on the ground and a group of United Arab Emirates extremists primed to take the blame. They will be found dead along with a businessman from Saudi Arabia. Incriminating paperwork naming the crown prince, Abdullah Bin Salman, will be discovered at the scene. At the same time, one of your supertankers in the Strait of Hormuz, The Texan Star, will be hit by an Iranian surface-to-air missile, pushing tensions to the brink of war.'

'Outstanding, General. While I feel for the loss of American life, once we are at war with the Middle East,

43

the oil industry will be in chaos. We can push the price of Texan oil through the roof while the Middle East is at war. During that time we will move our green energy solutions across the globe, cheaply and cleanly, killing off fossil fuels forever,' said the chairman, excited at the thought of his vision coming to fruition.

'Sacrifices have to be made, Mr Chairman, the planet has reached tipping point. If we don't do what has to be done, there will be no tomorrow for our children and children's children.'

'Thank you, General. All of us at the board owe you a massive debt of gratitude.'

The call disconnected and the chairman got up. He moved to a cabinet at the side of the room and poured himself a large whisky. Sitting back down at the large mahogany conference table, he swirled it around in the glass as he ticked things over in his mind. Downing it in one, he made a call.

'Yes,' came the answer almost immediately.

'Cheng Haku has outlived his usefulness, deal with him. The private jet is waiting for you at London City Airport,' said the chairman. He paused momentarily before adding, 'Good work at the Savoy.'

The line went dead without a reply.

After pouring another whisky the chairman made another call.

'Yes,' came the answer as quickly as the last.

'The police commissioner has everyone looking for the man and woman. I want you to find them first. Kill them and retrieve the package,' said the chairman hearing the line go dead the second he finished.

His temper got the better of him as he thought about Haku's incompetence. They all knew not to keep paper or electronic copies of their plans. Releasing his frustration, he threw the whisky glass at the wall, watching it shatter into thousands of pieces. Composing himself the chairman left the boardroom and walked over to an attractive woman in her mid-twenties.

'Take any messages please, Sandy, I'll be out all afternoon,' he said smiling.

'Improving your handicap, sir?' she said, smiling back.

'I will try my best, Sandy. Oh, could you get someone to clean up the boardroom, I broke a glass.'

'Certainly, sir, enjoy your game of golf.'

CHAPTER 12

With his baseball cap pulled down low and the collar of his jacket up high, Danny left Kate in the lounge area of the Star Inn opposite Vienna Central Station. He entered the train station walking confidently past the two officers at the entrance. He noted the black and white pictures of Kate and him on a piece of paper held by one of them. They paid him no notice as he bought two train tickets to Prague, departing from the airport station later that afternoon. Keeping his head low, he walked back out of the station, clocking two more officers on the other side of the station as he went. Kate smiled as he came through the hotel foyer towards her. He saw the tension lift in her face and realised how scared she was to be left alone.

'Right, I've got the tickets, but we must go through the station and get on the train to the airport separately, there are police offices looking for us travelling together,' he said looking at her reassuringly.

'I can't, I can't. What if they catch me? I…I—'

'Shh, it's ok. I'll be right behind you all the way. They

have a bad photo of you, black and white, with your hair down. We'll tie your hair back, keep your hoodie up, and walk confidently through the station. They won't give you a second glance, not if you're alone,' he said, putting his arm around her. As he comforted her, he eyed the hotel clerk on the reception desk over her shoulder, curiosity written all over his face as to who they were.

'Time to go,' said Danny.

They left out the front doors and stood across from the station. Danny smiled as Kate got herself together. She scooped her blonde hair back, tightly fixing it in a ponytail. He liked the fighter in her and couldn't help noticing how attractive she was.

'Just as I said, walk with your head slightly down. Look engrossed with your phone and walk straight to platform four. No one will bat an eye and I'll be following right behind you, ok?' he said as she flipped her hoodie up.

She nodded at him. Slinging her bag over her shoulder she walked towards the station entrance like any other commuter heading to work.

Good girl.

Cap low and collar up, Danny followed at a safe distance. Kate disappeared briefly as she passed through the station entrance. He picked her up again when he entered the station. He passed the police officers still looking for a man and a woman travelling together. They looked bored. He doubted they'd had surveillance training, or they'd have spotted them in an instant. His eyes scanned around the bright modern building with its shops and entrances, soaking in the mass of information with a well-practiced observation technique, allowing him to almost feel the surrounding crowd. He watched Kate pass through the ticket barriers and move on towards the platforms. As he passed through the barriers himself, an urgency of movement on the edge of his vision alerted him. A police officer moved in from the left, not running but moving with purpose in Kate's direction. Danny quickened his step, closing the gap as the officer got closer to Kate.

The platform was fairly quiet but not empty, leaving Danny with few choices. The officer got within a few feet of her, unaware that Danny was right behind him. He was a split-second away from being kidney-punched into the train carriage beside them, when Kate turned onto plat-form four and the officer continued straight on towards the platform toilets.

Slowing with a sigh of relief, Danny let Kate board the train. Without looking in her direction, he continued on and entered the next carriage. Once inside, he moved up the aisle until he could see Kate through the dividing door. She acknowledged him with a quick glance and a nervous smile. He sat so he could see her but stayed where he was and waited as the train filled.

The train finally lurched and ambled out of the station on its fifteen-minute journey to the airport station. Along the way Danny glanced between Kate and the views of central Vienna as it merged into the city suburbs before pulling into the airport train station.

Kate's eyes went wide when it stopped, locking onto his in panic. Danny stood calmly, smiled back at her and gave her a tiny nod to leave the train. She breathed deeply and pulled herself together. The two of them stepped off the train together from different carriages. They moved to the departures board to find the connecting train to Prague.

Danny noticed two groups of police on the other side of the ticket barriers. Luckily, they seemed intent on checking passengers coming in through the station, and not passengers crossing the platforms to get connecting trains. He let Kate lead again as they walked the two platforms to get on their train. Sitting apart, they waited through an excruciatingly slow twenty minutes until the train started to move. When the station faded into the distance, Danny moved up the carriage and sat down next to Kate.

'You ok? You did great, Kate,' he said.

In a release of stress and tension she flung her arms around him and sobbed. Caught by surprise, all Danny could do was hold her tight and wait for her to get it all out.

CHAPTER 13

Scott Miller got off the phone after calling every hospital in London. He'd finally found where they took Paul Greenwood after the explosion. The doctors at University College Hospital had managed to stabilise him, but due to a swelling on the brain they'd put Paul into an induced coma to help him heal. He was about to call Danny and tell him, when he heard the intercom buzzing by the front door of his luxury apartment. He clicked a button on the keyboard, closing the screen he was working on. Spinning around in his office chair he walked away from his computer, its multiple displays running through a fancy animated screen saver with Miller Software Inc displayed on it. Moving past the large lounge window with its panoramic view of the Thames and central London, Scott hit the intercom that linked to the block's secure entrance door.

'Hello,' he said looking at the camera feed of two stern-looking suited men.

'Mr Miller, this is Agent Denton and Agent Hooper

from MI6. We'd like to have a word with you regarding Daniel Pearson.'

The voice was official and the faces serious.

'Do you chaps mind showing your ID to the camera?'

Two arms shot forward and the blurry image of two MI6 IDs filled the screen. Scott left them hanging for a few seconds while he studied the image. He had no idea what MI6 identification should look like, but he didn't want them to know that.

'Thank you, gentlemen. I'll buzz you in, I'm on the eighth floor.'

Scott waited by the open apartment door until the agents exited the lift. He shook their hands and brought them through to the lounge, offering them a seat.

'Now how can I be of assistance?'

'Have you been in contact with Daniel Pearson in the last few days?' Denton said.

'Er, yes, briefly. We were supposed to go out for a drink when he came back from the Middle East, but he had to cancel. Unexpected business trip or something,' Scott said, keeping it as vague as possible.

'And you haven't spoken to him since? He hasn't sent or emailed you anything?'

'No, absolutely not, what's all this about?' he said, trying to sound a little impatient.

'Sorry, sir, I'm not at liberty to say, it's a matter of national security. If you hear from Mr Pearson we need you to get in contact with us immediately, ok? I have to warn you that withholding information regarding Mr Pearson will be viewed as an obstruction of justice and possibly aiding terrorist activity. Do you understand, Mr Miller?' said Denton, staring him in the eye while he handed him his card.

'Absolutely, I'll be sure to let you know if he contacts

me. Now if you don't mind, gentlemen, I have a conference call in five minutes,' Scott said, standing to show them out. He smiled at the door and shook their hands as they left. Just before they got in the lift he spoke.

'Oh, I've got an old friend in M16, fairly high up, field director or something—I haven't seen him for a while. Richard Jenkins. Please pay him my regards. I assume you know him?'

'Yes, sir, I know Richard Jenkins well. I'll be sure to pass them on,' said Denton without hesitation.

When they'd gone, Scott moved to the living room and watched out the large window until he saw them exit the apartments and drive off. He went to the office and grabbed his mobile. Selecting Danny's number, he was just about to dial when he paused.

MI6 my arse. They didn't even know it's Edward Jenkins not Richard. What if they have my phone tapped? What to do?

Scott grabbed his coat and left. Minutes later he emerged out of the underground carpark and gunned his Porsche down the road.

CHAPTER 14

An hour passed as the train sped through the Austrian countryside. Danny started to relax a little as they crossed into the Czech Republic. He looked over at Kate. She'd pulled herself together and smiled back at him.

She's tougher than she looks, I like that.

'Let's have a look at that package, Kate, see what all the fuss is about,' Danny said, gesturing for her bag.

She pulled the crumpled Jiffy bag out and gave it to Danny. He pulled it open and pulled out a rather unexciting external hard drive in a tough black rubber case, like something you'd use in the field or on location. As Danny spun it around in his fingers, he noticed a small green light built into the casing. It flashed in a split-second blip. He looked at it for a few minutes and it flashed again. After timing the regularity, he found it flashed once every five minutes. Not being a big fan of electronic devices that flashed, ticked, or had wires sticking out of them, Danny put it back in the bag, frowning. His phone broke his concentration, beeping the arrival of a message.

. . .

Dodgy chaps pretending to be MI6 asking about you.

I've bought this burned up phone. Call me when it's safe.

Just as he finished reading it, another message pinged into view.

It's Scott by the way.

Danny couldn't help chuckling at Scott's cloak and dagger messages, even though they sounded serious. He picked the number off the message and called Scott back.

'Scotty boy, it's good to hear from you, mate.'

'Quite. Are you ok, old man? I've had two serious-looking suits here pretending to be MI6. They were asking if I'd been in contact with you,' said Scott a little over-excitedly.

'Mm, how do you know they weren't really MI6?'

'I dropped Jenkins' name into the conversation but called him Richard. They pretended to know him but didn't correct me.'

'Ok that is odd. Edward's a senior agent, they should know him or know of him. Did they say anything else?' said Danny over the top of the train announcement for Brno station.

'Not really, just told me to let them know if you got in contact. What's this all about?'

'Information, Scotty boy. I was sent to pick up this weird hard drive and bring it back. At least three people have been killed to get whatever is on it, and half the Austrian police force have been after us to get it. Did you find out about Paul?'

'Yes. He's in hospital. They said he's only alive because he pulled a metal serving trolley in front of him as the explosion went off. The blast blew him across the room. He struck his head when he landed. They've got him in an induced coma until the swelling goes down. It's too early to tell if there's any permanent damage,' said Scott in a sombre tone.

'I'll keep my fingers crossed,' said Danny.

'You said it was weird?'

'Er, what?' Danny said, confused.

'The hard drive, you said it was weird, weird how?'

'Oh, it's in a tough rubber case like something you'd use in the field or military. It's got a little green light that flashes every five minutes.'

'Does it have S.T.E.D written on the bottom?' Scott asked.

'Hang on,' said Danny, pulling the unit back out of the Jiffy bag.

'Yep, what is it?'

'Satellite Trackable Encrypted Databank. It's made by Geotech. They do a host of trackable assets for the military. Anyone with login access can track it from anywhere in the world.'

'Shit, can I turn it off?' Danny said, feeling the train starting to slow for Brno station.

'Not without the login. The battery's designed to last for two or three days. I would suggest putting it into a metal container that will block the signal and make it untraceable.'

'If I get this to you can you get the information off it?'

'It may take me a while, but yes I can do it,' said Scott with his usual confidence.

'You're a star, Scott. I'm heading for Prague airport now. Stay on this number and I'll call you as soon as I'm back,' said Danny hanging up as the train pulled to a stop.

Kate had been listening and looked at him.

'Did he say they can track this thing?'

'Yeah, let's hope the bad guys don't know that. We need to get it in a metal container or... Does this train have a buffet car?'

'I think so, why?'

'I might be able to get some catering foil to wrap it up in,' he said getting up.

Kate followed him as he moved towards the back of the train. They reached the buffet car as the train began to move out of the station. Danny stood back as Kate spoke Austrian to the waiter. She smiled sweetly at him and he disappeared into the little kitchen, returning with a square of kitchen foil. She thanked him, passing the foil to Danny who promptly wrapped the hard drive up before tucking it back into the Jiffy bag and into Kate's bag.

'I'd have felt a lot happier if we'd done that back in Vienna, but at least no one can track us now. Let's go back to our seats.'

Moving along the train as it gathered speed, Danny slid the dividing doors open as he went. When he got to the door to their carriage, he froze with his hand on the handle. Looking through the window divide he could see the Chinaman two carriages down. He was moving slowly looking left and right at the passengers, his face showing the same unreadable blank it had back in Vienna.

Danny pulled his cap low and turned his back to him.

'Don't look, just turn and walk back. Now, Kate,' said

Danny, his expression changing to one not to be questioned.

She turned and headed towards the back of the train as instructed.

'That's good. Let's go, nice and calm. Keep going.'

'What is it?'

'The Chinaman,' he said bluntly.

'What are we going to do?'

'I'm working on it.'

CHAPTER 15

They'd entered the buffet car before Danny risked a look. He couldn't see the Chinaman but knew he wouldn't be far behind. Eyeing up the kitchen door, he was thinking of possible weapons, when the door at the far end of the coach opened and two men walked in. Danny instantly recognised the type: ex-military, lean and fit, every movement calculated, hard faces and alert eyes. Killers.

They locked eyes with one another. The man in the lead instantly went inside his jacket for a gun. Danny wrenched a briefcase out of a nearby passenger's grip and powered it into his attacker, knocking the drawn gun to one side. His body still spinning, Danny used the momentum and flow of kinetic energy to throw a full body weight punch with his right to the attacker's throat, dropping the guy to the floor, struggling for breath. Before Danny could turn back, the second man was on him: a quick combination of blows to his side before a lightning punch to his head.

Dazed, Danny fell back onto the terrified passenger

behind him. He blocked the next blow with the briefcase and kicked out hard from underneath it. His foot struck the guy hard in the balls. With a grunt he staggered back, allowing Danny to get upright and attack. Swinging the briefcase up, he slammed it into the man's face, dropping him.

A thud by his ear made him look at the case. A small dart was impaled in the leather. Following the direction it came from, he saw the Chinaman standing in the entrance to the carriage tucking the small blowpipe into his pocket. His arm moved with a lightning whip forward. The movement was so fast Danny didn't have time to think. Moving on instinct, he pushed Kate backwards into the galley kitchen door while he flicked himself backwards.

The glinting object cut the air between them, impaling the man Danny punched in the throat as he got up. It hit with such force that the man's head banged into the carriage door. He slid slowly to the floor, a look of surprise locked on his face and an ornate ivory-handled dagger protruding out of his eye.

Dropping with his full body weight channeled through his knee, Danny landed on the chest of the second guy. Hearing him scream as his ribs cracked, Danny reached down and picked up his dropped gun. He twisted to see the Chinaman hurtling up the carriage towards him. Before Danny could get a shot off, the Chinaman spotted the gun and leapt into the seating on one side of the carriage. Coiling like a spring, he pushed back off the hard seating and somersaulted back towards the exit. He moved quicker than Danny had ever seen before, zig-zagging between the seats on either side of the aisle before pushing and spinning through the carriage door out of sight. The movement couldn't have taken more than a couple of seconds and left Danny staring down the sights of his gun at the empty carriage door. When the Chinaman didn't reappear, he got up and pulled Kate out of the kitchen.

'We've gotta go. Now,' he said. Holding Kate's hand, he stepped out the far end of the carriage, over the dead attacker and his groaning colleague. Sliding the window down in the exit door, Danny looked out the train. It was going too fast to jump. He ducked back in to look through the glass into the carriage. No sign of the Chinaman but the passenger and buffet car attendant were on their phones. The injured attacker suddenly stood up and hurried down the carriage, holding his side as he went.

This is bad, we've gotta get off this train.

Looking outside again he could see the train track falling in to follow a busy road. He could see a truck station coming into view in the distance.

'Kate, when I say jump, jump and run for the truck stop, ok?'

She looked at him wide-eyed but nodded acknowledgement. Danny had one last look into the carriage then reached above the door and pulled the emergency stop lever. The train lurched as its brakes locked and the hundreds of tonnes of carriages started to slow. Opening the exit door, Danny gauged the speed. He didn't want to wait until it stopped as they needed to be up and away before they could be followed. Moving Kate in front of him, he waited for the right moment.

'Get read. I'm going to swing you out into that soft verge coming up. Just bend your knees and roll, ok?'

'No, no, I can't,' she panicked.

'Yes, you can. You can do it, Kate, I'll be right behind you,' he said as reassuringly as he could.

She looked back into his eyes as he gave her a wry smile. She kissed him unexpectedly and leaned out the door, holding his hand.

'One, two, three.' Danny swung her out and let go, pleased to see her land well and roll the speed off. Leaping out after her he did the same, running towards Kate and the truck stop. Looking back when he'd reached the fore-court, the train had a lot of carriages and was still moving slowly to a halt around half a mile away. He saw a door on the rear carriage open, and the Chinaman jumped down. He looked around, standing motionless when he spotted them, his expressionless face frozen in their direction.

The injured attacker jumped down clumsily beside him. He stumbled to his knees from the pain in his broken ribs. Without warning, the Chinaman reached inside his suit jacket and drew a knife. He sliced through the other man's throat as he struggled to get up. The Chinaman walked away, leaving the attacker with a stunned look on his face as he held his throat in a futile attempt to stem the crimson tide that flowed down his front. Seconds later he fell flat on his front, twitching. The Chinaman kept walking towards Danny and Kate, his eyes locked in their direction. No anger, no frustration, just an emotionless picture of a man who won't stop.

CHAPTER 16

D anny grabbed Kate's hand and led her through the rows of parked trucks. He gripped the gun hidden under his jacket with his other hand, instinctively releasing the safety, making it ready for use. He walked cautiously, tucking in tight to look round the front of each lorry as they passed from one row to another. They emerged on the far side, opposite the petrol station and services.

Danny spotted a British Pemberton Travel coach parked up with a group of young and middle-aged over-weight men in England shirts and scarves. They were chanting and singing as they piled onto the coach, carrying bags of booze and snacks. A patient tour operator in a blue blazer, tired of the endless singing and banter, ticked them off on a clipboard. Tucking the gun into the back of his trousers, Danny zipped up his jacket and led Kate over towards him.

'Good luck with that lot, pal, where are you off to?'

'Prague, for the England match tomorrow night. I

wouldn't mind but I don't even like football,' he answered with a grin.

'Look, I hate to ask but a lorry wrote our car off while we were in the services. We called a taxi but it hasn't turned up and we're desperate to get to her brother's wedding in Prague. Is there any way we could hitch a ride? I'm willing to pay,' said Danny.

Kate took the initiative and hung off his arm, looking suitably upset as she looked up at him with pleading eyes.

'Sorry, it's company policy. I just can't,' he said, tailing off towards the end when his spotted the fat roll of euros produced by Danny.

'Put that away, mate. Fuck off, Derick, we paid for this coach and we say they can have a lift. Right, lads?' said a short, fat man as he boarded the coach. A raucous cheer of approval boomed from inside.

Derick sighed and gestured for them to board the coach.
'Thanks...?'

'Ken, Ken Danbury, Chairman of Diddlesgate Social Club. I organised this little shindig, so I say on you get.'

'Thanks, Ken. I really appreciate this. I'm Matthew Freeman and this is my wife, Sue,' said Danny shaking his hand as they got on.

The coach was in good spirits, especially as a lot of spirits were inside the supporters. As the coach started to move, the lads shoved beers in Danny and Kate's hands. Danny smiled, raising his can thankfully. But all the time, his eyes scanned the truck stop for the Chinaman. Just as they pulled out onto the slip road to join the motorway, Danny saw him emerge from the line of lorries. He walked up and down searching the gaps between the vehicles before moving across and disappearing into the services. Thankfully, he seemed unaware of their location.

Danny relaxed and sat back. A flush of embarrassment hit him as he realised he was still holding Kate's hand. He would have let go, but she moved in close to him and tucked her head on his shoulder. They stayed that way as the coach and its noisy passengers headed their way to Prague. Watching the countryside fly past, Danny wasn't quite sure who was taking comfort from who. Either way, he didn't feel like moving.

CHAPTER 17

Cheng Haku sat in his office in the Macau hydrogen power plant. He clicked and permanently deleted file after file from his email folders. He cursed his own stupidity at not doing this after each one came in, and then cursed Jian Zhao's treachery for copying the files and selling them. Cheng was now on the chairman's bad side, which was not a place he wanted to be. Rumours of board members who had failed the chairman disappearing or having accidents—whispered their way through the remaining members with a chill.

But nothing would happen to me. I'm far too important. I pioneered the greatest contribution to the cause: clean power and water for all. No, no one would let anything happen to me.

The phone on his desk rang, snapping him out of his thoughts.

'Yes.'

'We have a high-pressure alert on number two nitrogen tank. The engineers are down there but can't find the fault. Should I shut the turbines down, sir?'

'No, no, we need a perfect report this month before roll

out. Tell them I'm on my way,' Cheng said grabbing his hi-vis jacket and hard hat on the way out.

The power plant was vast and split into two main buildings: one for the extraction of hydrogen from sea water; the other housed the four massive liquid-cooled hydrogen turbines. The process generated a massive amount of heat and it was necessary to use liquid nitrogen at certain stages to prevent a meltdown. Cheng's footsteps echoed down the metal staircase as he made his way to the plant generators. Exiting out of a side door, Cheng walked round the building past the massive hydrogen storage tanks shining white in the floodlit night sky. He entered a small hangar joined to the main building. Reaching the end of the section, Cheng put his pass card on an internal door and entered as it clicked green.

'Hello!' he shouted in the dimly lit room. It was empty apart from the four white 50,000 litre liquid nitrogen tanks.

He moved to tank number two and checked the dials. From somewhere in the dark he could hear a swishing sound.

'Hello, who's there?'

Cheng heard the swishing sound again with a brief glint of reflected light.

'Cheng Haku, you have lost the trust of the board.'

The voice was cold, unemotional, unforgiving, and instantly recognised by Cheng.

'No, no, the board can trust me. I will earn the board's trust. Tell the chair—'

'There's no going back, Cheng. It's time to face your destiny with honour.'

The voice was behind him now. Cheng spun around in panic. He caught a brief glimpse of the Chinaman spinning and slicing a three-foot Chinese dao sword through the air. It moved incredibly fast with martial arts perfection. The vision disappeared as the Chinaman stepped back into the shadows once more.

'Wait, I can straighten this out. Let me call the chairman,' Cheng begged, digging his phone out of his pocket.

A flash of glinting steel appeared out of the darkness beside him, disappearing so fast Cheng doubted that he'd really seen it. He looked back to dial the chairman and his face drained of colour as he looked at a bloody stump where his hand had been. Cheng cradled it to his chest and ran for the exit. He only got a few feet when the Chinaman flicked the blade across from a crouching position. The razor-sharp edge touched the back of Cheng's ankles before being drawn back, slicing through his Achilles tendon. Cheng fell on his front, screaming in pain and fear. His feet flapped helplessly to each side of him.

In sheer terror and with the primal instinct to survive, Cheng started crawl for the exit. The Chinaman stepped out of the shadows behind him. He sheathed the sword and tucked it inside his jacket. Reaching down, he spun the refilling cap off the liquid nitrogen tank beside him. Standing to one side, he turned the wheel that opened the valve to the tank. Gushing liquid poured onto the painted concrete floor, it bubbled and steamed as it crept its minus-196-degrees-celsius way towards Cheng.

The Chinaman vanished into the shadows behind the tank, reappearing seconds later in front of Cheng at the exit door. He crouched, watching without expression as Cheng desperately crawled towards him, tears streaming down his face. The bubbling, steaming liquid caught his feet first, freezing them to the floor. Cheng screamed in indescribable pain as the liquid sloshed around his legs; blood, tissue, muscle and bone froze solid in seconds.

In one last futile attempt to save himself, Cheng dragged and pulled himself forward as hard as he could, the bloody stump where his hand had been sliding smears of blood on the concrete. Cheng pushed himself up and stared defiantly at the Chinaman, his frozen torso snapping in half, slumping him forward. The liquid splashed around the front of him, freezing its way up. His mouth opened in a silent scream as his lungs froze. His head froze seconds later, locking him in a picture of pain and anguish.

The Chinaman straightened his suit jacket, turned and left the hangar, vanishing into the darkness once more.

CHAPTER 18

They arrived in Prague as the sun was setting. Derick dropped them off at the train station and they waved the supporters off to loud cheers and singing. They entered the station and Danny spotted the money exchange he was looking for. He changed all his Austrian euros into Czech crowns and went to the ticket office to ask for the airport. The ticket lady advised them in broken English that they would have to get the shuttle bus or a taxi as the train didn't go there. Danny thanked her, noting the odd look she gave them. When they got outside, he realized how they looked. Kate still had his slashed hoodie on and dirt-covered jeans from jumping out the train. He had dirt and a rusty blood stain on his jacket, with ripped and muddy jeans. Kate twigged what he was looking at and pulled the sweatshirt forward, poking her fingers out through the holes. She looked up at Danny and started laughing. It was the first time he'd seen her relaxed since they'd met; her face lit up and he couldn't help noticing how attractive she was. Looking at his watch and realising how tired and hungry he was, Danny decided it was time to get some clothes and get a hotel for the night.

'Right, come on, let's go shopping,' he said smiling back at her and taking her hand. They walked up the road until they came across Václavské náměstí, a long wide road with shops, bars and restaurants lining either side. He let Kate shop first, waiting patiently while she tried on outfits. Making their way along, Danny ducked in a shop and bought two cabin-sized suitcases so they wouldn't look out of place at the airport.

When Kate had finished, Danny's shopping took considerably less time; he spotted a Marks and Spencer and bought two pairs of the same jeans, two T-shirts and a new hoodie. Leaving with their shopping bags, they stopped in the first coffee shop they came to. Danny got changed in the toilets first, packing the rest of the shopping and old clothes into one of the small suitcases. He took the gun he'd got on the train and stripped it. Wiping his prints off it he put the bullets in his pocket. Lifting the cistern lid, he dropped the pieces inside. There was no point keeping it: he couldn't get it through the airport security. He'd drop the bullets somewhere safe and separate from the gun later. Kate smiled as he returned to the table a changed man.

'You look better,' she said, sipping her coffee.

Danny dumped the suitcase down and gave her a twirl.

'Right, your turn, off you go,' he replied, his deep brown eyes meeting hers.

As Kate disappeared into the toilets, Danny checked the hard drive was still wrapped up in tinfoil. The last thing he needed was to be tracked again. He'd just tucked it snugly into his rucksack when Kate returned. His unflattering hoodie was gone, replaced with a figure-hugging blouse and cardigan. He tried not to stare but couldn't help himself. Kate picked up on it, sliding into the seat beside him.

'I take it I look better then?' she said with a sparkle in her eyes.

'Eh, what, yes sorry, you look great,' he said, uncharacteristically flustered.

He googled hotels on his phone to move the moment along and came up with an impressive five-star one called The Grand Mark only fifteen minutes' walk away. They finished their drinks and strolled through the historical city. Danny slid the bullets out of his pocket and dropped them down a drain while he pretended to tie his shoelaces. Kate didn't notice as she admired the grand buildings. When they got there, the hotel was more impressive in the flesh than the picture. The doorman greeted them in his impeccable uniform and opened the door for them. They crossed the lobby and smiled at the woman on the reception desk.

'Good evening, do you have two rooms available?' Danny asked.

Kate tugged his arm and whispered in his ear, 'Danny, I don't want to be left on my own,' she said with a worried look on her face.

Danny put his arm around her shoulder to comfort her and turned back to the receptionist.

'Can I change that, do you have a twin room, please?'

'Sorry, sir, we only have suites left tonight.'

He looked at Kate.

'It's ok, we'll take it,' she said.

The suite was large and luxuriously decorated, with views across the city. Danny dumped his case and threw his rucksack on the large sofa.

'I'll sleep here, you take the bed,' he said chivalrously.

'Don't be silly, it's ok, I'm sure I can trust you after the last few days,' she said, dismissing the idea.

Danny just nodded before saying, 'I'm starving. Do you want to get something to eat?'

'God yes, I could eat a horse.'

They went down to the hotel restaurant. Kate was happy to take the stairs with Danny, especially after her encounter with the Chinaman in Vienna. They sat and ordered. Danny had the most expensive steak on the menu; Howard had got him into this mess, the least he could do was enjoy the money he'd given him.

They chatted. Kate told him about herself and her brother, Lee. Danny didn't talk about himself much: his past was chequered with the secrecy of the SAS and conflicts, and the pain and loss of his wife and child. The night went quickly by. He enjoyed Kate's company and after a little too much to drink they made their way back up to the hotel suite. He undressed to his boxers and climbed into the king-sized bed while Kate was in the bathroom. Taking off his trusty G-Shock watch he put it on the bedside table and plugged his phone into the charger. He sat back in bed and tried not to stare as Kate walked back in. She was naked apart from her bra and lace knickers; her body was smooth and toned. Her eyes were locked onto his as she climbed on the bed, her long blonde hair falling down seductively around her shoulders.

'Are you sure about this?' he said in a whisper.

She smiled and straddled him, putting her hand through the unruly hair on the back of his head. She pulled him close and kissed him passionately. Emotions stirred inside him as he put his arms around her and held her tightly to his body. She ran her hands over the scars on his back and kissed him on the neck. Turning her, he put her gently on the bed. He slid her lace knickers off as she hooked her hands inside his boxers and pulled them down. The two of them moved in unison, the tension and emotion of the last two days being released as they moved faster and faster, breathing heavily until they came together. Kate gasped as she looked in his eyes. She smiled to see that the intense look Danny usually wore had softened. Cupping his face, she kissed him passionately again. When the moment eventually passed, Kate held him tight for a long time, eventually rolling to one side.

'Are you ok?' Danny said, still holding her.

She nodded, wiping a little tear away. They spoke no more. Danny just held her until they both fell asleep.

CHAPTER 19

A faded, rusty, blue transit van pulled into the car park of the Courtyard by Marriott hotel. It drove to the far corner where the driver killed the engine and lights. The Chinaman turned in his seat and reached down into the back of the van. He gripped a tarpaulin and pulled it up past the handles of the wire garrotte deeply embedded in the van owner's neck, past his open mouth and swollen tongue, past his terror-stricken, wide, staring eyes until it covered him. Satisfied, the Chinaman got out, locked the door and tossed the keys into a nearby hedge. He moved along the edge of the car park, invisible in the shadows, careful that the car park cameras hadn't picked him up leaving the van. He didn't worry about wiping it down to cover fingerprints. He didn't have any—they'd been lasered off years ago. He didn't worry about DNA—his wasn't on any file anywhere in the world. He made his way to the hotel entrance, walking past a Pemberton Travel coach as he went. He approached the receptionist. She looked up with minimal interest at the forgettable, expressionless Chinaman in a forgettable black suit. He spoke in perfect English, with as few words as needed to be said.

'Good evening, I'm looking for the tour operator for the Pemberton Travel coach outside.'

'Certainly, sir,' she said tapping on her computer.

'Erm, Derick McCrindle. Would you like me to give Mr McCrindle's room a c—'

She stood frozen in mid-sentence, her mouth open, her eyes moving in confused panic. The Chinaman slipped his tiny blowpipe into his pocket and pulled the little neurotoxin poison dart from her neck, tucking it safely into its tube on his bracelet. He reached over and spun her computer screen round as her breathing faded to a whisper. Noting the room number, the Chinaman spun the screen back. The receptionist lost consciousness and dropped to the floor behind the desk. Moving around the desk, the Chinaman picked her up under the armpits and dragged her into the back office. He sat her gently in the chair. Her heart had stopped and he doubted she had any awareness of her surroundings. He took her master key card off the bunch clipped to her belt and paused before leaving. Reaching carefully forward, he put his fingers on her eyelids and closed them shut.

Outside the office the bell rang on reception. The Chinaman calmly straightened his jacket and walked out the office.

'Good evening, sir, how may I help you?' he said with the faintest hint of a smile.

'Good evening. I just need to hand my room key in,' the man said, handing it across the desk.

'Thank you, sir, I hope you enjoyed your stay with us.'

'Yes thank you, very nice. Goodbye,' he said with a wave as he dragged his suitcase out the exit doors.

As soon as he was out of sight, the Chinaman walked into the lift and pressed the button for the fourth floor.

Fifteen minutes later his phone vibrated silently in his pocket.

'Yes.'

'Have you eliminated the man and the Crossman woman?'

'No, he is proving more...resourceful than anticipated,' the Chinaman said.

'Where are they now?'

'Their last location was the train station in Prague. It is likely they took a train to Germany—Nuremberg or Leipzig, maybe Munich,' he said sliding a long needle-like blade out of Derick McCrindle's nose. He'd pierced his frontal lobe and expertly twisted it around, lobotomising Derick and robbing him of his ability to move, communicate or retain a memory. He sat lost, locked in his own world, never to come out of it.

'What is your next move?'

'They will be heading for the U.K. I will get a flight tomorrow and intercept them when they arrive in London.'

'He has made this the top priority; I will join you the day after tomorrow.'

'Very good, brother. I will see you when you land,' said the Chinaman hanging up. He wiped the blade with a tissue then wiped the trickle of blood from Derick's nose. Standing up, he flushed the tissue and left the room. Derick sat on the floor with his back against the wall, staring into space, dribble rolling down his chin.

CHAPTER 20

The light through the hotel curtains woke Danny up. He reached for his watch to check the time, careful not to wake Kate who had her head on his shoulder and arm across his chest.

Half seven, still early.

He put the watch back and turned to look at Kate. Her shiny blonde hair covered half her face as she slept. She was a very attractive woman in a natural way: not heavily made-up, no false nails. She had a strength and guts he really liked. Her eyes flicked open as he watched, taking a second to focus on him with her deep blue eyes. She smiled softly at him before pulling herself close. The feeling of how much he wanted her surprised him as he responded to her touch. She moved on top of him and they made love again. They showered together when they'd finished and then headed down for breakfast.

'So what's the plan?' she said while eating croissants.

'We'll get a taxi to the airport and get some tickets for the U.K., but not a London airport—they'll be waiting for that. I want to find out what and who we're dealing with.'

'How are you going to do that?'

'I need to get Scott to find out what's on that hard drive,' he said, gulping down his third cup of coffee.

They finished breakfast and returned to the room to pack up their carry-on suitcases. Danny risked a look at the hard drive. The light had stopped flashing, which he guessed was because the battery had finally gone flat. He took the foil off and packed it into the case so it wouldn't look odd when they X-rayed it at passport control. They checked out and got the concierge to get them a taxi to Václav Haval Airport. The journey lasted forty minutes and took them though the picturesque historical city centre and out to the green and leafy suburbs before the airport came into sight. They entered the departure terminal and made for the airline desks.

Danny looked relaxed and calm, putting his arm around Kate to guide her to the sales desk. Inside he was tense. His eyes scanned the crowds, noting the exits and cameras and airport police. He almost took two of them out on a reactive instinct as they appeared from behind the desk area directly in front of him. Their eyes locked, but there was no sign of recognition or alert. They moved to one side and carried on their way. Shaking it off, he smiled at the woman on the KLM desk and asked what flights she had available for the U.K. Their luck was in: there was a flight for Norwich Airport in forty-five minutes; just enough time to get through passport control, walk to terminal two and their gate number. Danny paid in cash, thanked her, and made his way with Kate to passport control.

The Chinaman entered Václav Haval Airport. He walked to the easyJet check-in and showed his e-ticket to the man on the desk. Smiling politely, the easyJet man asked if he'd had a nice time in Prague. The Chinaman returned his enquiry with an unemotional, 'Yes.' It ended the conversation dead. He proceeded to passport control with his secure metal carry-on case in his hand. Stepping up to the baggage scanner, he put the case on the conveyer belt to go through the X-ray machine and stepped through the metal detector. Five metres ahead of him, Danny and Kate picked their cases off the end of the conveyer belt. Danny turned and froze, looking eye to eye with him. The Chinaman moved forward, desperate to follow them as they disappeared around the corner into the departure lounge.

'Sir, sir,' came a voice from behind him.

He turned without answering to see two airport security guards beckoning him over to his case.

'Could you open the case for me please?' he demanded, albeit politely.

The Chinaman rotated the combination locks and flicked the case open. The guard's eyebrows raised as he viewed the assortment of ornate knives and daggers and throwing stars.

'Antiques—a precious collection,' he said unflustered.

'Ok, that's fine, sir, but you will have to go back to the check-in desk and check them into the hold. You can't transport these in hand luggage,' he said closing the case and escorting the Chinaman back towards check-in.

———

Moving as quickly as they could, checking behind them as they moved through the shops, snack bars and coffeehouses of the departure lounge, Kate looked scared and Danny had to hold her back to stop her running.

'It's ok, he's not behind us,' Danny said close to her ear.

'How did he know we were here? We're going to get arrested or killed. I can't do this.'

'Shh, he didn't know we were here, it's just a coincidence. He's here to get a flight. Ok?' said Danny, putting his arm around her and pulling her close.

'He's still not there. Let's get out of the departure lounge and to our gate. He's got no idea where we're flying to.'

She pulled herself together and nodded at him. Danny took another look behind them. The Chinaman still hadn't come through to the departure lounge yet, so they walked swiftly to their gate.

Sitting with their backs to the wall, they faced the entrance to the gate without speaking. The minutes ticked by slowly until the call to board the plane came over the tannoy.

CHAPTER 21

Gentlemen, we have retired Cheng Haku from the board. With 80% controlling interest in Haku Industries, we have taken operating control of the project from Cheng's brother, Zahang Haku. I'd like to welcome new board member Donald Sinclare to the table. He and a management team are flying out tomorrow to take over the running of the plant,' said the chairman to the faces on six of the screens in the boardroom.

They met the news with cautious murmurs and nods of approval.

'If there's no further business, I suggest we reconvene tomorrow night at twenty hundred hours GMT. We have a big day ahead of us tomorrow, gentlemen. The start of a chain reaction that will save this planet is upon us.'

As the screens went blank one by one, the chairman muted all but one before speaking.

'Not you, Lord Ravenmere, I need a moment of your time.'

The chairman waited until the last of the other screens terminated their connection before continuing.

'Our little problem in Vienna is still a problem. The Chinaman says he and the woman caught a plane from Prague airport, destination unknown, but in all probability back to the U.K. I want them found and dealt with. Do you understand me, Hubert?'

'Yes, of course, I'll get everyone on it. Our contact in MI6 has discovered the identity of the man with Miss Crossman. His name is Daniel Pearson, an ex-SAS soldier and one of Howard's private acquisitions. It won't be long before we locate them,' said Lord Ravenmere rambling.

'Just get it done and report back to me. Listen to me, Hubert. Under no circumstances can that information be allowed to surface.'

Lord Ravenmere's mouth opened to say something else, but the chairman cut the screen off before it came out. He was in no mood for polite conversation. He rubbed his forehead. The enormity of what he was trying to do was weighing heavily on his shoulders. The chime of an incoming video call caused him to sit back and take note.

Bloody Africa and its greedy and corrupt states, polluting and ripping everything from minerals, diamonds, oil and gas from the earth, without a care for its workers or the environment.

'Mr Mambosa, I sincerely hope you have some good news for me,' the chairman said with a weary sigh.

'I'm sorry, my friend, I do not. The president's adviser took offence at your proposals to move green technology ahead of their current resources. He wanted me to tell you to keep out of his affairs and out of his country.'

'That jumped-up little tyrant! Let's see how the bastard likes another Ebola outbreak in his shitty country,' the chairman said, a little angrier than he intended.

'Are you sure that's the best course of action?'

'The time for talking has passed; it's time for action.

We have to bring his country to its knees. I want him begging for our help.'

'Very well, I will continue talks with Sudan and Somalia to see if we can make headway,' said Mambosa.

'Thank you, my friend. I'll have the bio department ship the virus as soon as possible. If the president caves, we will of course send vaccines and aid workers to help.'

'Ok, I will talk to him again when his people are demanding action and he is most under pressure.'

The video call went dead, leaving the chairman alone in the quiet boardroom.

CHAPTER 22

The plane descended across the Norfolk fields, touching down gently on the tarmac at Norwich International Airport just after midday. Danny and Kate walked across the tarmac to enter the arrivals hall in the small terminal building. The two officers at passport control showed no interest in them as they passed through. Danny scanned around but didn't see anyone suspicious waiting for them as they came through to the main building. Spotting a money exchange, Danny changed up his diminishing foreign currency for sterling.

'Shall we get a hotel room?' said Kate, pointing over at the Holiday Inn across from the terminal.

'We will, but not around here. If they track us, the first place they'll check is hotels surrounding the airport. We'll get a taxi into the city centre and find a hotel there,' he said with a reassuring smile.

Kate smiled back and followed him to the taxi rank. Just being back on English soil made her feel a hundred times better. On the taxi driver's recommendation, he took them to the historic Maids Head Hotel in the old part of the city centre, near the cathedral. Danny paid for the room in cash and signed in under a false name. Seeing themselves to the room, Danny made a call while Kate freshened up.

'Hi, Scott, I'm back in the country.'

'Welcome home, old boy. Have you sorted your latest conundrum out yet?' asked Scott, checking out of his apartment window.

'No, I could do with a little help with that one,' said Danny, glad to hear his friend's voice again.

'What do you need?'

'Have you ever been to Norwich, mate?'

'Can't say I have, but I have the feeling I will be shortly,' said Scott with a chuckle.

'I need to know what's on this hard drive everybody's so desperate to get hold of.'

'I must admit, so am I, old boy. There's been a dodgy blue plumber's van outside my apartment building ever since the phony MI6 men left. I know they're a lazy lot, but they haven't even got out of the van.'

'I'll text you the address, Scott. Drive about a bit first, mate, make sure you're not followed.'

'Ok, I will. I'll come up in the morning. Oh, by the way, Paul's awake. He's still bashed up but they've taken him off the critical list and he should make a full recovery.'

'Thanks, Scott, that's great, mate. I owe you one.'

'No change there then. Bye for now.' Scott rang off.

The MI6 men and surveillance van worried Danny. Whatever information was on that drive, it had some very big players worried.

'Who was that?' said Kate, coming out of the bathroom.

'A friend of mine, Scott. He'll be up in the morning to find out what's on that hard drive.'

85

'Oh, ok, I thought we'd just go to the police with it,' she said, a frown spreading across her forehead.

'Once I know what's on it I'll have a better idea of who to take it to. Don't worry. I'm as keen as you to make this someone else's problem,' Danny said giving her a reassuring smile.

'Glad to hear it. I just want to get back to my normal, boring little life,' she said, her face relaxing a little.

'You will. Anyway, that's tomorrow. What shall we do tonight?' Danny said with a cheeky grin.

CHAPTER 23

The van door creaked as it opened. He handed his colleague one of the bacon rolls and one of the coffee cups he'd balanced on the rusty blue roof while he opened the van's passenger door. Picking up his own cup, he got in and slammed the door shut.

'Did you put sugar in this?' said Milton.

'Yeah. Anything happen while I was out?'

'Er, no, other than he's up early today,' Milton replied pointing up at Scott's apartment and Scott opening the bedroom curtains.

'Christ, it's all go around here. Three fucking days we've been watching this guy. What's the deal?'

'You know as much as I do, watch him and report any contact with the targets,' he said, tapping the black and white pictures printed out on an A4 sheet of paper.

'Huh, seems pretty pointless to me.'

'Listen, Doug, I'm going to let that go because you're new. But take my advice, we're paid to do a job, no questions, no fucking moaning, ok? If Lord Poncy Fucking Ravenmere wants us to clean his toilet, we clean his fucking toilet. Got it?' said Milton, the annoyance clear on his face.

'All right, all right, sorry I fucking spoke,' said Doug taking a big bite of his bacon roll as he looked out the front windscreen brooding. He was taking a big swig of coffee when Scott's Porsche appeared out of the underground car park.

'Oh shit, here we go,' said Milton, starting the van.

Scott turned towards them. He got within fifty metres and floored the twin-turbo Porsche 911. It gunned past them in a flash, doing 0 to 60 in less than three seconds.

'Shit, shit,' Milton cursed, lurching the van forward and back trying to do a three-point turn.

'Agh, fucking hell. You fucking twat!' shouted Doug as scolding hot coffee went all down his front.

'Shut up, you prick!' Milton shouted back, revving the bollocks off the van in a futile attempt to catch the sports car.

Over half a mile ahead of them, Scott's car disappeared around the corner. Milton screamed the van after him, reaching the corner a good thirty seconds later. Scott's Porsche was nowhere in sight. Cursing, Milton reluctantly pulled over to a stop. Doug sat muttering under his breath, trying to blot coffee out of his top with a serviette. They both looked at each other, Milton's face flushed with anger.

'Not a word, don't you say a fucking word.' As the van fell into an awkward silence, he pulled out his phone to call it in.

CHAPTER 24

After the usual scrutiny from customs over his antique knives and weapons, the Chinaman—with his legitimate antiques cover business and acquisition paperwork—walked freely out of the customs area and into the arrivals hall at Heathrow. His identical twin stood motionless by the exit, watching without expression as his brother approached. Stopping a few feet apart they faced each other, mirror images except for the case in the hand of one of them.

'Brother,' they both said in a monotone greeting.

'Have they been located?'

'No, they didn't fly into any of the London airports. Come, I have a car waiting. He has arranged for assets to be at our disposal and Lord Ravenmere's contact is using all of MI6's resources to find them.'

His brother nodded his approval and the two of them walked side by side out of the terminal building.

Danny and Kate sat in the centuries-old glass-covered courtyard of the WinePress Restaurant in the hotel. Danny had one ear on Kate and the other on a TV playing the morning news. He was on his second plate of full English breakfast when a report caught his attention.

'We have to interrupt the sport for a breaking story. We're going live to our overseas reporter, Alex Giddeon in Baghdad. Alex, what can you tell us about this morning's attack?'

'Yes, Nick, around 8 o'clock this morning, Iraq time, five men armed with automatic weapons forced their way into the American Embassy here in Baghdad. Early reports suggest that ten American diplomats have been killed, along with four Iraqi civilians working at the embassy. The situation changed around twenty minutes ago when a joint American and Iraqi special forces operation located the terrorist cell. The operation resulted in a firefight and the deaths of five men from the United Arab Emirates. We will report more on that as information comes in. We have further news from the Middle East that an American supertanker, The Texan Star, has been struck by an Iranian missile in the Strait of Hormuz. American Naval forces are en route to assist the vessel which has no power and is leaking its cargo of crude oil through its ruptured hull. With relations in the Middle East already at an all-time low, these latest events could push America to breaking point.'

'Looks like they're going to war,' Danny said, clearing his plate again.

'Surely it won't come to that, will it?'

'I wouldn't be surprised if it does, tension's been building for months. The U.S. has been building troop numbers in neighbouring Iraq and half the U.S. Navy are already in the Gulf,' he said, distracted by the phone buzzing. Looking at it he smiled.

'Scott's on his way, he'll be here in about an hour.'

'Great, perhaps we can finally find out what this is all about,' she said looking at Danny open-mouthed as he got up to get more toast.

'What? I can't help it if I worked up an appetite last night,' he said grinning as she blushed.

CHAPTER 25

ooking out of the window in their room, Danny spotted Scott's white Porsche approaching down the historically-named Tombland. It passed the 900 year old arched entrance to the cathedral before turning into the hotel car park. Danny left Kate and went downstairs to meet him. Walking through he smiled to himself. He found Scott leaning on the desk, chatting up the receptionist.

'Is this man bothering you, miss?' Danny said, creeping up behind Scott.

'Ignore him, my dear, he was dropped on his head too many times as a child,' said Scott brushing his floppy, sand-coloured hair back. Winking at her, he grinned with a set of pearly-white teeth.

She smiled back, a little embarrassed, as Scott turned to his friend.

'Good to see you, old boy. Shall we have a look at your little problem?' he said, patting the laptop bag slung over his shoulder.

'Absolutely, mate, come on up,' said Danny heading off up the stairs, leaving Scott facing the lift doors.

'Of course the stairs,' sighed Scott turning to follow him.

Walking into the room behind Danny, Scott put his bag down and saw Kate sitting on the bed.

'Oh, hello, my dear, and who might you be?' he said, extending a hand.

'Kate,' she said, extending her hand to meet his.

Scott took it and kissed the back of it instead of shaking. Danny rolled his eyes.

'Don't mind Scott, he's looking for the next ex-Mrs Miller.'

'It's a pleasure to meet you, Scott,' she chuckled.

'The pleasure's all mine, my dear. Now if the caveman's ready, shall we have a look at this hard drive?'

Danny shook his head with a smile and grabbed the hard drive out of his rucksack. Scott cleared a space on the little table and set up his laptop. He got a set of tiny screwdrivers out of the laptop bag and started unscrewing the tough casing. When it came apart he unplugged the solid state hard drive and took it out. He discarded the case on the armchair in the room's corner and turned back. Attaching plugs and cables from his bag to the laptop, Scott's fingers danced over the keyboard as he worked on accessing the encrypted drive.

'Any joy, Scotty boy?' Danny said, watching over his shoulder.

'Have patience, Daniel. This is a 256-bit encrypted drive. It will require some time and room service to crack. Coffee and croissants or pain au chocolat will do very nicely, thank you. I missed breakfast this morning.'

'No problem, mate. I'm on it,' said Danny, picking up the phone in the room.

In the chair behind him, the jolt and warmth from the radiator caused the flat battery in the hard drive case to release a last remnant of power. The little green light blinked, as it emitted its final tracking signal.

———

In a disused warehouse in central London, Doug and Milton sat around sparring jokes and banter in typical ex-military style with two more of Lord Ravenmere's assets, Ray and Andy. The Chinamen twins sat upright in silence on an old sofa, to one side. They looked straight ahead, unmoving, waiting. When one of their phones went off, he reached slowly into his pocket, pulled it out and answered.

'Yes.'

'We've had a GPS ping on the package.'

'Where?' he said in a monotone voice.

'Central Norwich, Norfolk. I'm sending you the location now. We only received one ping before it disappeared, so accuracy is restricted to a half-mile square.'

The Chinaman heard the ping as the location arrived in a message. He didn't speak to the caller again. He just hung up and showed the message to his brother. After reading it they stood in perfect unison and straightened their suit jackets.

'Load up.'

'We move. Now,' they said, interrupting the group.

The team got up and started collecting their stuff, quick enough—but not too quick. As mercenaries and hired killers, they didn't like to bow to anyone's orders too quickly.

'Now. Let's move,' said one of the Chinamen.

'All right, Chinks, keep your hair o—' said Doug, instantly regretting it. The Chinaman's brother had a ten-inch blade at his throat with such speed he hardly saw him move.

'Ok, ok, I'm moving,' said Doug backing away with his hands up passively.

'Prick,' said Milton.

They got into three separate black Land Rovers. With the Chinamen in the lead, they moved off in convoy through the London traffic.

CHAPTER 26

anny paced up and down the room like a caged
tiger. He was never very good at the slow stuff.
He was much better at tackling problems head-
on and hard. The inpatient desire to know who he was up
against was driving him mad. Turning the TV on to pass
the time, Danny sat down next to Kate as the news
came on.

'Thank God for that, old boy, I thought you were going
to wear the carpet out,' said Scott still tapping away in
between finishing off the last croissant.

'How are you getting on, Scott?' Danny said in return.

'Not long now, ten or fifteen minutes at a guess.'

'Leave Scott alone to do his thing,' said Kate putting
her arm around him.

'Right, yes. Sorry,' Danny said turning his attention to
the news on the TV.

'Tension is growing between America and Saudi
Arabia after documents discovered in the raid of the
American Embassy in Iraq unearthed links to the Saudi
Arabian crown prince, Abdullah Bin Salman. In other

news, UNICEF are sending workers and medical supplies to Sudan to help an Ebola outbreak in a town called Wad Madani. Lastly, Cheng Haku, the world's leading hydrogen energy pioneer, died in a freak accident at his prototype power station.'

'Never one to blow my own trumpet, but this genius has cracked your little hard drive,' said Scott with a smug look on his face.

'Never doubted you for a minute, Scotty boy,' said Danny leaping off the bed, Kate close behind him.

'What have we got, Scott?'

'Let me see, it would appear to be a copy of someone's email folder. Erm hang on, yes. From somebody called Cheng Haku. Let's see what he's been up t—'

'Sorry, Scott, did you say Cheng Haku?'

'Yes, why?'

'He's just been on the news, killed in a freak accident at his power station,' said Danny, leaning over Scott's shoulder to see the emails.

'Mm, the man who forgets to delete his top-secret emails, gets them copied and then dies in a freak accident. Rather suspicious I must say. Let's delve deeper, shall we?' said Scott, excitement growing in his voice.

Scott started opening streams of emails. Most of them were addressed from someone called the chairman and a variety of names @theboard.com copied in. The subjects started innocently enough: lots of deals and meetings in Africa to pilot hydrogen electric power stations and supply clean water in Somalia, Sudan and Libya, with a second-phase plan for Western African states. As the emails went on, things got more sinister: the board's plans to scale up the supply of natural resources after someone assassinated Somalia's opposing minister for the environment; a large payment to the President of Sudan to attain mining rights;

a later email discussing the President of Sudan taking the money without honouring the deal.

As they read on, the following emails from the chairman said he'd sent negotiator Mambosa Botwa in to convince the president that he should honour the deal with the board. Two days later there was an email instructing their pharmaceutical company to up production, and a shipping document from them for a biohazard package to Sudan.

'Jesus, they've just done it—released the Ebola virus. The bastard will kill thousands,' said Danny reading on in disbelief.

'Open that one please, Scott,' said Kate with a shaky voice.

Scott opened the email with the subject, *Containment*. It started off with the chairman berating Haku over his stupidity. He told him that Jian Zhao and the journalist Lee Crossman had been taken care of. Haku returned the email expressing how happy he was about this, only to get a furious reply explaining how Lee Crossman had posted the package to his sister. The chairman went on to tell Haku the matter was now out of his hands; Lord Ravenmere had stepped in, using his Vienna contacts and the company's security unit to retrieve the package and take care of an unknown asset and Kate Crossman.

'Where have I heard that name before?' said Danny.

'Lord Hubert Ravenmere is a leading member of the House of Lords, fourth generation of Ravenmeres, very old school network,' said Scott, smiling at his own knowledge.

'How do you know that, mate?'

'The House of Lords has a very secure internal network: website, portals, email addresses, that sort of thing. They are a very good client of mine, one that requires me setting up the members' access, logins and emails. Lord Ravenmere's quiet the cantankerous old git and a very good friend of Michael Davis, the chief of the Secret Intelligence Service.'

'Well that explains what Howard was worried about, and the explosion that took him and Paul out,' said Danny more to himself than the other two.

'Quite. Er, who's Howard?' said Scott.

'That's a very good question. He is, or he was, the man in the shadows that protected this country from people like this.'

Scott continued to open more files until he came upon one sent to all members of the board: *The Reformation of the Middle East.* It contained a presidential war plan by General Harley Buchanan, the President of the United States' military adviser. It also contained details of land, sea and air strikes to Saudi Arabia in retaliation for the attack on the American Embassy in Iraq. The document went on to plan strikes in Iran for their attack on ships traveling through the Strait of Hormuz.

'This is crazy, how is that possible? The attack on the embassy only took place last night, I heard it on the radio driving up this morning,' said Scott looking at Danny confused.

'They've been planning this for a long time, Scott. What does the rest of it say?'

Scott scrolled down to read the rest of the files; pages and pages of global reform, wind power, solar power, hydrogen electric... the list went on. Once the key players were in place in the Middle East, Africa, China and Russia, the board would move in for a trillion dollar plan to cover the globe with green energy technology, ending the use of fossil fuels completely.

'No wonder they want to get their hands on this,

there's going to be a lot of people asking a lot of very awkward questions about this,' said Scott, closing the laptop.

'What do we do now?' asked Kate.

'We find someone we can trust to expose these bastards,' said Danny sitting back on the bed, thinking.

'Any idea who?' said Kate.

'I need to get to London to talk to Paul, run this by him.'

'How about I take us all for a spot of lunch, old boy, then I'll drive you to London,' said Scott packing up his stuff.

'It could be dangerous, Scott.'

'Fantastic. Count me in,' replied Scott with a big grin on his face.

CHAPTER 27

General.'

'Mr Chairman.'

'Let me congratulate you on the perfect execution of the embassy plan. How is the president taking it?'

'I have the president's trust and he's following my recommendation for the escalation of naval forces in the Red Sea and Persian Gulf. As we speak, 200,000 troops are being mobilised into Iraq.'

'Excellent, and what is Saudi's reaction?'

'As expected, the royal family is taking the hard line. If they don't see a step down in U.S. troop activity, the crown prince has stated he will take it as a declaration of war.'

'They're not refuting the embassy attack?' the chairman said.

'No, they refuse to comment on matter, as predicted.'

'Excellent, General, and you are ready for the next move?'

'Yes, sir, we have an asset in place. The prince is sched-uled for an official visit to Medina on Wednesday, at which time we will assassinate him. When they do their search, they will find an American sniper rifle on a nearby rooftop. We anticipate air strikes on our naval fleet in retaliation.'

'Thank you, General, outstanding as always.'

The screen went black. The chairman sat back in his chair rubbing his forehead. Still no news from England. Pressing a speed dial button he called Lord Ravenmere.

'Hubert, give me some good news,' said the chairman without humour.

'Mr Chairman, the assets are closing in as we speak. I am confident we will have the situation contained very shortly,' Lord Ravenmere said with self-assured arrogance.

'I don't want to hear about your confidence. Very shortly, Hubert, I want to hear it's done,' he said, his voice rising in anger before cutting Hubert off before he could reply.

CHAPTER 28

Scott, Danny and Kate had lunch in The Glass House pub just down from the hotel. Scott's continuous enthusiasm lifted both their spirits until they almost forgot the trouble they were still in. Danny patted his jacket pocket for the fifth time, checking the hard drive was still safely tucked away. There was no way he was letting it out of his sight.

'Right, let's get you two lovebirds back to London, shall we?' said Scott winding Danny up.

Kate blushed as Danny gave him a mock deathly stare.

'Ignore him, he's probably been working on that one since he arrived at the hotel,' Danny said winking to Kate.

The minute the three of them walked out the pub, Danny clocked Doug and Milton walking down the centuries-old cobbled street opposite the pub. He recognised the type: faces that had seen action, hardly noticeable bulges under the left-hand side of their jackets. He tried moving Kate and Scott towards the hotel without being spotted, but Scott stared obviously across at them, attracting instant eye contact.

103

'Danny, that's the two guys from outside my apartment.'

'I've already seen them, just keep walking. Go, go,' he said ushering them forward. He took a glance to see them following at a distance. Doug was on his phone.

Shit, we're going to have company.

'Keep going past the hotel, over there, through the arch to the cathedral grounds.'

They crossed the road walking as briskly as they could without running. They turned in through the high flint walls and medieval gate that surrounded the cathedral grounds. Looking around, Danny tried to work out the best course of action. To his left was a row of centuries-old buildings running a hundred metres or so to another medieval gated entrance. In front of them lay a large lawned green with the cathedral entrance on the opposite side.

'Over there. There's got to be a back way out through the cathedral,' he said pointing them towards the huge open doors with an imposing stained-glass window towering above them.

Danny turned as they headed for the doors, spotting Ray and Andy coming in through the far gate, the same look as the others, the same slight bulge under the jacket. Glancing directly behind him, he saw Doug and Milton coming through the same gate they had. Danny looked left before entering the cathedral, scanning the grounds to see if there was another way out. He cursed under his breath at the Norwich School sign and pupils milling about in smart uniforms. With his options narrowed he hustled Scott and Kate into the cool grandeur of the cathedral's main hall, where huge pillars drew their eyes down its length. As they looked up, archways on top of archways rose to the high ornate ceiling.

Danny led them off down the left-hand outer passageway that ran outside the pillars. From a bird's-eye view, the cathedral was a cross-shaped building with ornate tiered oak pews at its centre where the choir sat. This was hidden from view of the cathedral entrance by a small arch and a walled section under the cathedral's huge piped organ. Danny looked through the arch, spotting Doug and Milton walking slowly up one side of the cathedral while Ray and Andy worked their way up the other. Each one had their hand tucked inside their coat, gripping a concealed weapon. Danny ducked back and scanned the area behind him. There were several doors and alcoves in the top part of the cathedral. Wasting no time, he started trying them all.

'Scott, Kate, try that side.'

After a run of locked doors, he found a door by the altar unlocked. It opened into a tiny chapel with a high-backed, ornately painted altar, depicting Jesus on the cross. Danny looked behind it. It had a narrow gap leading into a small space directly behind it. Danny leaned back out the door.

'Scott, Kate, over here,' he said trying not to shout. He hustled them in and led them to the gap behind the altar.

'Slide in behind there. Don't come out until I return, ok?'

Kate was going to protest but Danny's face was as hard as the stonework around them and his eyes glinted with the same deadly determination she'd seen on the train.

'Come on, my dear, let Daniel do what he does best,' said Scott. Nodding to Danny, he took Kate's hand and squeezed himself into the small gap, out of sight. Danny left them. After a quick look around the door he slid out, closing it silently behind him. Using the alcoves and pillars as cover, he worked his way towards the main section of the cathedral and the enemy.

CHAPTER 29

Peering along his line of sight down the far side of the main hall, Danny watched Doug split off from Milton and move out of sight between the pillars. As soon as a group of tourists ambled off towards the gift shop, Milton pulled a silenced pistol from under his jacket and continued moving in Danny's direction.

Keeping low, Danny scooted past the choir seating and climbed up the steps to a carved wooden pulpit. He grabbed a heavy leather-bound bible off its stand and looked over the edge. Seeing Milton edge his way through the arch, Danny bobbed down out of sight. Counting the steps until Milton passed under the pulpit, Danny leaped over the top, powering the edge of the heavy book into Milton's neck. The blow made him crumple to one side. Ignoring the pain, Milton fell back on his training and elbowed back into Danny's ribs. The blow knocked Danny back far enough for Milton to flick the gun around. As he pulled the trigger, Danny jammed the bible over the end of the gun. Three soft pops went off in quick succession, blowing a cloud of leather and paper into the air.

Grabbing the silencer with his free hand, Danny twisted the gun outwards, snapping Milton's trigger finger out of its socket as it went. Gritting his teeth through the pain, Milton punched Danny hard in the kidneys with his left, following it up with a blow to the head at lightning speed. Dropping the gun over the pews, Danny blocked Milton's last blow and dived forward with a headbutt. It shattered the bridge of Milton's nose, dazing him in a cloud of pain and stars before the eyes. Danny took the initiative and threw himself over into the choir seating. Pushing down with all his weight, he wedged Milton into the tight space between the wooden pews until he was unable to move.

Danny pummeled Milton with blow after blow. As Milton fought to get his arms up, Danny saw the gun lying under the seating behind him. He reached back and grabbed it. On instinct, Danny brought it round and was just about to pop Milton when footsteps coming through the arch stopped him. Grabbing one of the thick prayer cushions off a seat, Danny push it over Milton's groaning face. As a group of Japanese tourists came through, Danny went down on his knees, jamming one across Milton's chest, trapping his arms down, and the other across his neck choking him. The Japanese group ambled around clicking off endless photos. Danny placed the gun down out of sight and crossed himself before putting his hands together as he pretended to pray.

The seconds passed endlessly. Muffled moans disappeared as Milton convulsed and suffocated under the cushion. The movement below Danny ended and the tourists finally moved off out of sight. Holding the gun under his jacket, Danny came down from the pews and moved through the arch to the left side. Taking a look towards the front of the cathedral, Danny's eyes locked on Ray's. He was twenty metres away. A young mother stood between them holding her baby.

Time stood still. Ray stared at Danny. Danny stared at Ray. Each had a hand under their jacket holding a gun. Ray was itching to draw his.

Don't do it, don't you fucking do it.

The tension was unbearable. Danny was willing the mother to leave. If Ray drew his gun, she'd be killed in the crossfire for sure. Out of the corner of his eye he noticed an exit to the cloisters. There was a sign above Ray that also said the cloisters. Danny looked Ray in the eyes and cocked his head in the exit's direction. Taking a quick glance, Ray resumed eye contact and gave a small nod of agreement. They moved in unison, eyes never breaking focus until they moved through their individual archway into the cloisters.

The ancient covered walkway with its rows of pillared arches formed a square around a lawned garden. Danny entered at one corner as Ray appeared at the opposite end. With no one around they both drew their guns and spun behind pillars. Danny took a darting look down the outside along the grass. He moved fast towards the next pillar. Seconds before he reached cover, Ray leaned out and took a shot. Chips of sandstone splintered past Danny's ear as he tucked behind the pillar. Keeping up momentum, Danny rolled to the inside and sprinted forward, his gun in front of him steady as a rock. He tucked back in when he was halfway down the cloister and closer to Ray. Flattening himself against the back of the pillar, Danny slowed his breathing and concentrated on the surrounding sounds. He was sure Ray would think he was still taking cover two pillars back.

Movement—which side? Breathing. Where? Inside.

Ray's gun came into view as he advanced along the

inside to where he thought Danny was. Grabbing Ray's wrist, Danny pulled it towards him violently. The speed and power of the pull shattered Ray's elbow as it snapped around the pillar. His agonised scream didn't have time to leave his mouth as Danny popped three rounds into his chest at point-blank range. He caught Ray as he dropped. Dragging him out through the arch and sitting him on a bench in the garden, Danny balanced him in the corner like he was resting. He took a quick look around, making sure no one was around, then tucked Ray's gun in the back of his trousers.

Leaving the cloisters, Danny slipped silently back into the cathedral. He scanned the pillars and walkways but couldn't see Doug or Andy in the main hall. A knot formed in the pit of his stomach when he thought they might be near Scott and Kate. Moving faster and less cautiously than he should have, Danny scooted from pillar to pillar in a fast sweep. Look left, look right, duck out and go to the next. He passed the cross-section with the pews for the choir and tucked in behind the next pillar, giving him a view of the top hall.

Still no sign of them.

Danny moved out to go to the next pillar and came face to face with Andy. They instinctively grabbed each other's wrists, each man holding the other's gun out of their line of fire. Andy was smaller than Danny but younger and at his physical peak. Their arms strained as they used every ounce of strength to move their own gun in for the kill. They stared at each other with murderous intent, faces hard, cold and determined.

The barrel of Andy's gun started moving a millimetre at a time towards Danny's head. Andy's mouth twitched up into an evil grin as his confidence grew, convinced he had the upper hand. Gritting his teeth, Danny went in for a headbutt. Andy saw it coming and moved his head back enough to take the power out of the blow. Danny only managed to split Andy's lip as he moved off-balance. Andy planted a boot in his stomach, kicking them both backwards off each other. As they split, suppressed pops of gunfire sounded as one in the single moment. Danny got hit in the chest as he put a bullet through the centre of Andy's forehead. They both landed flat on their backs, feet apart, motionless.

CHAPTER 30

From behind the altar, Scott and Kate heard the heavy oak door to the chapel creak open. They both held their breath instinctively; the more they tried to be quiet, the more every minute movement felt like a fanfare announcing their position. Light footsteps approached and the faint sound of steel being drawn against steel made their hearts pound like a drum roll. Kate's eyes went wide as the Chinaman's face came into view through the gap between the wall and the altar.

He stood as he'd done before, no expression, cold dark, unreadable eyes staring at their prey. He held a foot-long knife in each hand, the wavy blades glinting their ornate snake engravings towards them. He slowly pointed one of the blades towards Kate. In an explosion of movement, he launched towards them, his blade lined up with Kate's throat. With nowhere to go, Kate watched the blade slice towards her. When it got within inches of her throat, the side of the Chinaman's head disintegrated, spraying the wall with a sickening splat of blood, bone and brain matter.

Kate and Scott stared in disbelief as the Chinaman flopped to the floor, lifeless, the space where he'd been, empty, until Danny moved into view, gun in one hand, clutching his chest with the other.

'Come on, let's go,' he said in a pained voice.

They slid out, stepping carefully over the Chinaman's body and the pool of blood creeping its way across the flagstone floor.

'Are you ok?' said Kate, shocked to see the bullet hole in his jacket.

'Yeah, I'm just bruised,' Danny said pulling hard drive out of his jacket pocket, a mangled bullet embedded deep into the middle of it.

'Bloody hell, old man, that's incredibly lucky—or incredibly unlucky, depending which way you look at it,' said Scott grimacing at the remains of the Chinaman's brains sliding down the wall.

'No time for that, Scott, there's at least one more out there. Let's go. I've found an exit,' Danny said.

Taking Kate's hand, he peeped around the door. With no one in sight he led them behind one of the alcoves to find a heavy oak door. Opening it they squinted at the burst of sunshine as they exited by the vestry. A footpath led away to an arch through the back of the cathedral grounds.

—————

His footsteps were steady; his appearance impeccable and calm as always. He glanced over the choir's pew at the body of Milton wedged on the floor. Looking up the line he saw the dumped body of Andy. His expression remained neutral as he carried on through the cathedral.

The Chinaman entered the chapel with Doug following closely behind, his eyes nervously looking around as he went. The Chinaman didn't falter at the sight of his brother's body. He squatted down on his haunches, carefully picked up the curved snake daggers and stood up.

'Excuse me, gentlemen, I'm about to give a small service in Saint Luke's Chapel.'

Doug jumped, turning to see the reverend standing in the doorway in full regalia. The Chinaman turned slowly, giving the reverend full view of his brother's bloody body and the glinting dagger in each hand.

'My son, what has happened? What have you done?' said the reverend, the colour draining from his face. He watched the Chinaman walk towards him, the shock rooting him to the spot. The Chinaman stood in front of him, arms by his side, his face expressionless, unreadable, and his eyes cold and dark staring at him. In the blink of an eye, his face contorted with rage as he punched the daggers into the reverend's chest. Once, twice, four times, so fast you couldn't count. The reverend didn't feel any pain. It felt as though he were stuck in time, unable to breathe or move, a scarlet stain oozing down his white robe.

The Chinaman crossed his arms, so the daggers sat either side of the reverend's neck like scissors. With a yell he released an inhuman amount of speed and power, slicing the reverend's head off its shoulders. As the body slumped, the head rolled across the flagstone floor. The Chinaman's composure returned immediately. He dropped to his haunches once more and wiped the daggers clean on the reverend's robe before slipping them inside his jacket. He stepped over the body, walking towards the main entrance to the cathedral, Doug nervously following a few steps behind him. Walking out into the sunshine, they headed for the medieval archway and exited into Tombland. Behind them, screams echoed eerily around the vast open space of the cathedral as the bodies were discovered.

CHAPTER 31

Members of the board, we are at a pivotal point in our quest. Once the crown prince, Abdullah Bin Salman, has been eliminated and they have discovered the American sniper rifle, the Saudi authorities will return the body and rifle to the capital. Ballistics will match the bullet to the gun, and we expect immediate retaliation with air strikes on the United States naval fleet in the Persian Gulf. On the other side of the Gulf, the United States Navy has entered Iranian waters to protect The Texan Star, which drifted over the border while they undertook engine repairs. When Iranian jets arrived on the scene, the U.S. Navy reacted by shooting one down. Iran has released a statement: they deny the missile attack on The Texan Star and consider the shooting down of their jet as an act of war. The president has approved General Buchanan's war plan and thanks to Lord Ravenmere, we have a majority agreement from the Prime Minister's cabinet for U.K. military support. Once Saudi declares war, U.S. air strikes will commence on Riyadh and Shiraz simultaneously. At the same time, combined U.S. and U.K.

naval forces will cut off the Strait of Hormuz choking off the oil supply chain from the Middle East,' said the chairman, barely containing his excitement at the success of his plans.

'Mr Chairman, what is the situation with Cheng Haku's information leak?' stammered a nervous-looking man on one screen.

'That, Malcolm, is all in hand,' said the chairman, slightly annoyed.

'Is it? My sources tell me you missed your target in England and left a city in a terrorist lockdown,' said Malcolm, pushing further.

'The situation is under control. Our assets underestimated the target. It will not happen again.' The chairman's voice rose with his anger. His eyes burned through the screen at Malcolm, unnerving him enough to drop the subject.

'Now if that's all, we will reconvene on Wednesday evening after the Prince of Saudi has been eliminated. Hubert, if you could hang back a minute, I need a word.'

The board disconnected one by one until only Lord Ravenmere remained.

'Tell me you have this under control, Hubert?'

'It is, my contact in British intelligence has hacked the GPS unit in the car the target and his friends are travelling in. They are heading down the M11 towards London as we speak. Additional assets have been notified and are awaiting despatch when we have their destination,' said Lord Ravenmere with an air of smugness.

'Good. Do not mess this up, Hubert. Let me know the minute it is done.'

CHAPTER 32

Damn it,' said Danny, pulling the slug out of the middle of the hard drive.

'Look on the bright side, old chap—it saved your life,' replied Scott as he drove out of the Blackwall Tunnel, heading around the A205 towards Tooting, St George's Hospital, and Paul.

'Is it ruined?' said Kate from the back.

'Well, it's an SSD as opposed to HDD, which is in our favour.'

'Scott, talk to me like I don't know what the hell you're on about, which I don't,' said Danny, managing a smile.

'Ok, ok, sorry. It's a solid state drive, so inside there will be ten NAND flash memory chips that share all the stored information. Hopefully the bullet will have only damaged some of the chips. I know a man who can lift the chips and access anything that's survived.'

'Great, we'll go and see him after we check in with Paul.'

'Let me call him first, old boy, he's a rather interesting character and he doesn't like strangers, ok?'

'Whatever you say, Scott,' said Danny feeling happier at the thought that they could salvage some information.

Traffic was heavy as they crossed South London and it took them nearly an hour to get to the hospital. Danny had Scott drive past the car park twice before he felt safe enough to park up.

'Stay here a sec, Scott, keep the engine running,' said Danny, stepping out of the car.

He stood with his hand under the back of his jacket, firmly gripping the gun tucked into his belt as he scanned the cars and then the hospital entrance. Nothing visible or sub-conscious set his instinct for trouble on edge.

'It's ok, let's go,' he said, ducking down to Scott.

Kate got out to join Danny as Scott fetched his laptop out of the boot.

'You never know. The hard drive might, by some miracle, still work,' he said.

Taking his hand off the gun and relaxing a little, Danny walked to the entrance with Kate and Scott close behind. Everything in reception looked normal, so Scott went to ask where they could find Paul Greenwood.

'He's in a private room on the fourth floor,' said Scott pressing the button to call the lift.

'We'll take the stairs,' said Danny and Kate simultaneously before looking at each other and laughing.

'Ok, if you insist. I don't see what's so funny though.'

'You had to be there, Scott. I don't think I'll ever get in a lift again,' said Kate, heading up the stairs.

———

Outside, two black vans entered the hospital car park within seconds of each other. They split and drove to either side before parking to face the hospital entrance. The engines died, but no one got out. Their tinted windows obscured the occupants from prying eyes.

———

After poking his head in to check out the corridor, Danny led the others to Paul's room. He looked inside to find Paul sitting up in bed reading a newspaper. His head had a bandage on it and the side of his face was purplish-black with bruising. He looked over the top of his paper with a bloodshot eye. Flipping it down, he smiled at the sight of Danny and Scott.

'I wondered when you'd turn up,' he said to Danny, smiling.

'Charming, and there's me thinking you might actually be hurt. Some people will do anything to get out of work.'

'Mm, I'll ignore that comment. Scott, nice to see you again, and this must be Kate. Lovely to meet you, my dear. So let's hear it. I might have had a nasty blow to the head, but I'm still guessing you had something to do with the headline news. Five dead and a terrorist alert at Norwich Cathedral.'

'Five? I only killed three and the Chinaman,' said Danny shrugging before continuing. 'It's bad, Paul, worse than you or Howard could have dreamed of. These bastards are trying to start a war in the Middle East.'

'You must tell me everything. As for the Chinaman, you got one of them. While you were dealing with the one in Vienna, what I'm assuming is his twin was responsible for the bomb that killed Howard and nearly killed myself here in London.'

They sat around the bed and filled Paul in on the events of the past few days and the information on the hard drive. He sat and took it all in. Paul had been an analyst and a top intelligence operator in the military before leaving to start up Greenwood Security. He was the smartest person Danny knew and was extremely well-connected with several government agencies.

———

Two large Range Rovers pulled into the hospital car park. They didn't split. They parked close to Scott's car, the passengers in each vehicle getting out. They stood out all dressed in black, a variety of baseball caps on their heads partially concealing the earpieces in their right ears. Wrap-around sunglasses covering their trained, alert eyes, and a suppressed stubby sub-machine gun hung under their baggy jackets from shoulder straps. They stood alert, watching over the car park while one worked the lock on Scott's car. He was in within seconds, checking the interior. He came out, shut the door and moved round to check the boot. Seconds later he shut it, shaking his head to the driver of the Range Rover.

After a command through the earpiece, their heads moved in unison towards the entrance to the hospital. Seconds later they worked themselves through the cars towards the entrance doors. At the same time, the van nearest the Range Rovers opened up its side door on the blind side to them. Four people got out, armed and dressed in police anti-terrorist unit uniform. They approached keeping low from behind. Splitting two to a car, they neared their targets, throwing the driver's doors open in perfect synchronisation. The lead shoved a gun in the driver's face while putting a finger to his lips as they pulled their earpieces and radios off. A quick go-command and the other van door opened. Four more armed officers exited and sprinted to the hospital entrance. They swept in from either side of the doors, assault rifles raised, catching one of the Range Rover passengers standing guard by the stairs.

'Armed officers! Down on the ground. NOW!' shouted the two lead officers as patients screamed in the waiting room.

The guy at the stairs swung open his jacket, raising his sub-machine gun in a defiant effort to wipe out the officers. He didn't get far: the two officers shot him with a tight cluster of bullets to the chest before he leveled his gun.

CHAPTER 33

S hh,' Danny said. From the fourth-floor room, he turned his ear towards the door.

'What? I don't hear anything, old boy,' said Scott puzzled.

Danny pulled the gun from the back of his trousers and headed for the hall.

'Stay here until I get back. Can you walk, Paul?'

'Yes,' Paul replied already climbing out of bed.

'Get dressed. I've got a feeling we'll be leaving in a hurry.'

With that, Danny slipped out into the hall. The long corridor had a set of stairs at either end. Although he was sure he'd heard gunfire, he couldn't tell where it had come from. He took a guess and moved stealthily towards the main stairwell they'd used to come up from the hospital reception. As he got close, he could hear footsteps—light, moving quickly as they made their way up the stairs. He slowed his breathing with his back against the wall, out of sight to anyone coming up the stairs. Tensing himself to take out the enemy as they got to the top, he waited, listening. The noise of the door opening opposite caused him to flick his gun round in surprise. With his eyes locked down his gun sights, he found himself looking into the eyes of a terrified nurse. Before she could scream, Danny put his fingers to his lips and signalled for her to go back inside. She backed up, shaking, her eyes flicking towards the stairwell just before the door closed.

Shit, too late.

The gunman darted into the corridor before Danny could turn to fire. In that crucial heartbeat, Danny pushed the attacker's gun against the wall. The impact caused the gunman to pull the trigger. The bullet ripped along the corridor wall, exploding a light in a shower of glass. The gunman was well-trained and quick. He grabbed the barrel of Danny's gun before he could put a bullet through his eye, wrenching it backwards out of Danny's grasp while powering a knee into his ribs, winding him with its speed and power.

Resisting the reflex action to double-up in pain, Danny folded his arm and whipped the steely bone of his elbow into the man's temple. The blow hit so hard his head flew to one side, striking the corridor wall with a heavy thud. His eyes glazed over as he dropped, Danny sighed as the image of a second gunman emerged from the stairs in front of him. Thinking quickly, he gripped the falling man's jacket with one hand and ripped the gun out of his hand with the other. He yanked him upright with all his might, blocking a barrage of fire from the accomplice. The body jerked and shook as the gunman opened his eyes, regaining consciousness and losing his life in the same terrifying second. As they both fell backwards to the shiny floor, Danny aimed to one side of the dead man, squeezing a couple of rounds off. The first ripped the gunman's ear off, shattering the earpiece; the second found its target in the centre of his forehead.

Rolling the body off him, Danny got to his feet, slipping in the blood. He darted his head down the stairwell. Spotting movement two floors down and grabbing a gun off the floor, he raced back down the corridor towards Paul's room, a gun outstretched in each hand. As he got close, the barrel of a sub-machine gun appeared from the far stairs, with a slither of a gunman's face visible behind it. In slow motion Danny fired at the tiny target. The gunman already had Danny in his sights, and he expected to feel the burning hot rounds hit him at any second. Instead, the gunman's head jerked to one side as the side of his head exploded onto the wall of the corridor opposite like the splat of a modern art piece. Fighting the confusion at the scene in front of him, and with the sound of hurried footsteps approaching behind him, Danny stretched his arms apart, a gun pointing to either end of the corridor. Whipping his head back and forth between the sound of footsteps from both sets of stairs, Danny spotted a head dart around the far stairs for a look. It flew back out of sight as Danny squeezed off a round, blowing plaster off the wall where it had been.

'Whoa, stand down, Danny, we're here to help,' said a familiar voice from the other stairs.

'Tom?'

'Yeah, it's me—Tom,' he said, poking his head around the corner.

Danny relaxed and dropped the guns to his side. He'd worked with Tomas Trent a few years ago as part of a special task force set up by Paul Greenwood and MI6 to stop a group of terrorists from attacking London and New York's financial systems.

'Ok, boys, evac and clean up. Five minutes. Go,' Tom

said moving into full view, puzzling Danny with his police terrorist unit uniform.

Noticing, Tom just said, 'Necessary subterfuge, mate.'

More uniformed men came up from both staircases. The lift door pinged open and suited men wheeled two trolleys out. They had *Coroner's Office* on the back of their jackets. They didn't waste a second zipping the bodies into tough black body bags. As Danny and Tom moved to Paul's room, the bodies were being wheeled back into the lift and two more guys came up the stairs, arms loaded with cleaning equipment.

'Thank Christ,' said Scott when Danny and Tom came through the door.

'Tom?' said Paul, shaky, but up and dressed.

'Good to see you both again. I will explain all, but for now I need to get you out of here before the real anti-terrorist squad turns up.'

They moved to the corridor as the cleaners finished cleaning the blood off the floors and wall. They bagged the last of the cleaning materials into thick refuse sacks before hurrying down the stairs. Danny relented, breaking a golden rule, by going down in the lift to support Paul in his weakened state. One of the other uniformed men joined Tom at the exit to the hospital.

'Site is clear. CCTV's been erased, sir,' he said as a van pulled up in front of them.

'Witnesses?' said Tom.

'Ten. All told it's a matter of national security and made to sign a gagging order.'

'Thanks, Brian, that should keep the police confused for a good while.'

The side door of the van slid open to reveal a long, padded bench seat fixed down the middle. They helped Paul in and sat down themselves. The side door shut and the van pulled away before their backsides had barely touched the seat.

'Ok, Tom, what's going on?' said Danny.

'I will answer all your questions shortly,' said the man in the passenger seat as he turned to face them.

'Edward Jenkins, so nice to see you again,' said Paul to his old friend.

'Is this an MI6 operation?' said Danny surprised.

'Not exactly. We'll be at the safe house soon. Everything will be explained.'

CHAPTER 34

After following the GPS signal from Scott's car all the way from Norwich, Doug and the Chinaman arrived at the hospital just as Edward Jenkins' team was leaving. They parked up on the side of the road overlooking the car park and watched. Fake coroners and cleaners moved out of the hospital as fast as they could, bundling body bags and bin liners into a van before climbing in and driving off hastily. It was replaced at the entrance by a second van. The Chinaman's body tensed at the sight of Danny, Scott, and Kate helping Paul into the back.

'Who the fuck is that guy? He's got more lives than a bloody cat,' said Doug, astonished.

'Shut up. Follow that van,' said the Chinaman, watching the van leave.

'All right, all right. Fucking hell, who stole the jam out of your doughnut?' said Doug, cutting up a car to drop in behind the van.

The Chinaman sat motionless apart from a flash of anger crossing his face at Doug's remark. They'd only followed for half a mile before a Tesco home delivery van pulled out sharply from a side road, cutting into the gap between Doug and the van.

'Christ, what's this twat doing?' said Doug about to honk the horn.

'Don't,' said the Chinaman raising his hand. 'It's a countermeasure to stop anyone following.'

'Bollocks, it's just a delivery van,' mocked Doug.

A row of parked cars narrowed the road to a single lane for twenty metres. The Tesco van pulled across to go through when there was a gap in the oncoming traffic. It got halfway past and stopped abruptly in the middle, blocking the route. Doug could just make out the driver exiting the van and running forward. He wound the window down and stuck his head out to get a better look just in time to see the driver jumping into the van they were following, before driving off out of sight.

'Fuck,' said Doug pounding the steering wheel.

'Take me to the warehouse. I need to call in.'

CHAPTER 35

After driving for twenty minutes, Edward instructed the driver to do a few diversions to check they weren't followed. Satisfied, they drove straight to their destination in the affluent Dulwich Village, London. Pulling up to a property with a high wall surrounding it, Edward pressed a button on his key fob and the strong wooden gates opened silently inwards. A large, impressive new build, all glass, metal and wood, came into view; it must have been worth 10 million or more in this part of London. They parked at one end of a sweeping drive, next to the other van from the hospital and two large Audi 4x4s.

The house was open-plan with the lounge to one side of the hall. The staircase spiralled round to the first and second floors, which led the eye up to an ornate glass atrium and a huge modern chandelier hanging down its centre.

They moved through to a huge kitchen-cum-dining room with large side-to-side glass bi-folding doors that looked out onto a patio area and an immaculately-tended garden.

'This is a bit out of your pay grade, isn't it, Edward?' said Danny giving Edward a grin.

'I should bloody well hope so,' came a voice he recognised from behind them.

'Howard,' Danny said, turning with the rest of the group.

Howard moved into the room in an electric wheelchair, his left leg in plaster below the knee and his right arm and hand heavily bandaged and hanging in a sling. He had a dressing on the right side of his face from his cheek and temple to behind his ear.

'It's good to see you, Howard,' said Paul, limping slightly as he moved forward and shook his friend's hand.

'The feeling's mutual, Paul.'

'How the hell did you survive the explosion?'

'Due to the nature of our recent meetings, I thought it prudent to take precautions. My suit was Kevlar-lined, and I was wearing body armour under my shirt. I've lost two fingers, but apart from a broken leg and some burns, I'm very glad to be alive.'

Howard moved through them to the dining area before turning.

'Right, while the team change and tidy up from today's little adventure, let me get you all some refreshments and then we can have a little catch up.'

While they waited, Danny checked on Scott and Kate sitting on two of the twelve chairs surrounding the large limed oak dining table. They looked a little lost and detached from the trained professionals moving around them.

'You two ok?' he asked, putting a hand on Kate's shoulder.

'I suppose so, old boy. I was a tad concerned about my

car. The parking ticket's run out and it's probably clamped by now.'

Danny couldn't help but grin at Scott's concern; nevermind the bullets and hired killers, what about his car?

'I don't see what you're grinning about,' Scott said, frowning.

'Sorry, Scott, I'll talk to Edward and get someone to sort it. You all right, Kate?'

She nodded a yes but he could see the stress and shock of the last few days was wearing her down.

'Don't worry, we're safe here,' he whispered in her ear.

After a few more minutes the team started to float into the room and take positions around the table. Most had changed into casual jeans and T-shirts or hoodies, except Edward Jenkins, who'd changed into a dark grey suit over a white silk shirt and tie. Howard positioned himself at the head of the table, his loose jogging bottoms and top looking out of place on the usually impeccably dressed man of mystery.

'Ok, gentlemen and lady, let's get started shall we?' said Howard, waiting until the room quietened down before continuing.

'Just for our esteemed guests I'll recap on the events of the last few days. After my apparent untimely demise in the restaurant explosion, I was whisked away to a private clinic by my men to get me patched up. We know the board has people inside the government and MI6, so I brought Edward in, as his history with Paul and Danny puts him above reproach. He already had his suspicions that someone at the top of MI6 was hampering proceedings for his or her own gain. Edward introduced me to Tomas Trent, who most of you already know from the cyber-attack business with Marcus Tenby a few years ago. Half the team is from Tomas's old unit, off the books of course.

The other half, like Mr Pearson here, has been personally selected for their discretion and unofficial talents in the field. I'm hoping the information Mr Pearson retrieved from Vienna will shed some light on the organisation we know as the board.'

Howard finished and all eyes moved down the table as he gestured to Danny to continue.

'We might have a slight problem with that,' said Danny pulling the hard drive out of his jacket pocket and placing it on the table. The deep indent in the middle from the impact of a bullet was clear for all to see.

'On the plus side, it saved my life after I ran into a little trouble in Norwich,' he said in an attempt at levity as Howard frowned and faces fell.

'Gentlemen, I have a little of the information still on my laptop and have read much of the contents. I also have a contact who specialises in data retrieval. I'm sure he will be able to salvage a decent percentage of the information.'

'Ok, thank you, Scott. No point crying over spilled milk. Let's go to damage limitation. We'll get you to your contact as soon as the meeting adjourns. What can you tell us about the information you've seen?'

Scott immediately got his laptop out, flipped it open and started tapping.

'Do you need the wifi password?' asked Howard.

'Not necessary, dear boy. I hacked that on my phone two minutes after we got here,' said Scott with a certain amount of smugness.

'Regarding Edward's suspicions, we have two names. The first one is a board member, Lord Hubert Ravenmere. A member of the House of Lords and very influential, he is also very good friends with Michael Davis, the chief of the Secret Intelligence Service.'

'Davis, that makes sense. He's stonewalled several of

my investigations, insisting on dealing with it personally. He also took charge of the investigation into the explosion that nearly killed you and Paul,' said Edward to Howard and the group.

'Go on,' said Howard.

'I haven't got a copy left on here, but we found a recommended war plan from General Harley Buchanan, the president's war adviser. It was in retaliation for the escalation of events in the Middle East and written before the attack on the embassy in Iraq happened. The board is manipulating events to start a war across the Middle East. When we looked further, the board has key members all over the globe. It is even responsible for releasing an Ebola epidemic in Sudan to put pressure on its president for mining rights. The aim of the board seems to be the global eradication of fossil fuels and world domination in all aspects of green energy generation and distribution.'

'The big question is, who is behind this?' said Howard, looking intensely serious as he digested the information.

'Unfortunately, we didn't find out who that is in the files we opened. He's only ever referred to as the chairman. I assume he's American because of the spelling of colour, and the reference to time zones,' said Scott closing the laptop and sitting back.

'Thank you, Scott. The revelations regarding the Middle East must take precedence. We can't let this group cause death, pain, and suffering on an unimaginable scale for personal gain. Let's get you to your man. We're going to need something concrete if we are to take to this to the President of the United States. Thank you, gentlemen. We will take an adjournment while I consider the best course of action.'

Howard finished and everyone dispersed to resume

their various duties. Howard moved his wheelchair over to Scott, Danny and Kate.

'Who is this data guy, Scott? Can we bring him here?' said Howard.

'Not a chance, old boy, he's rather an odd little man. He's a bit sensitive about his name so he goes by the nickname Byte Lord. He's a bit of a conspiracy nut and rather paranoid. No offence but he wouldn't trust you guys. It's best I go to him.'

'I'll go with him,' said Danny.

'Me too,' said Kate quickly, not wanting to be left with strangers.

'Ok, Tom will drive you wherever you need to go. There's a secure phone in the lounge. Take that —my number is already programmed into it, and Danny, get a shoulder holster from the other room; we can't have you running around with a gun hanging out of the back of your trousers,' said Howard dismissing them immediately as he scooted around indicating for Edward and Paul to follow him. Plans needed to be made.

CHAPTER 36

The chairman sat in a high-backed leather chair at the top of the boardroom table. He looked tired and pale. The strain of the last few days was taking its toll. On the screen in front of him was the expressionless face of the Chinaman. Speaking in a quiet, calm monotone voice, he recounted what he'd seen at the hospital. Finishing without personal comment, he fell into silence waiting for the chairman's instruction.

'Sit tight and await instruction,' the chairman said. There was an unusual hesitancy in his voice before he continued. 'I'm sorry about your brother.'

The Chinaman stared through the screen as if waiting for something more, causing an awkward silence before giving a curt nod, followed by a blank screen. Slightly taken aback, the chairman took a deep breath and tapped a few keys. The centre screen burst into life with the words *Trying to connect* displayed across its middle. The chairman drummed his fingers impatiently on the table as he waited, his anger and frustration building with every excruciating second that passed. Finally, the screen expanded with Lord Ravenmere's face looking sheepishly back at him.

'Mr Chairman,' he said, trying his best to sound and look confident.

'Twelve assets lost, and the situation is not only not contained, we have another unknown party involved and in possession of unknown information that could ruin us all. Tell me something worth hearing, Hubert,' said the chairman, his temper growing as he finished speaking.

'I... I... I've got Davis on it. Neither MI5 or MI6 know who these people are. This man, Pearson, has taken out all the assets we have available. I'm sorry, I don't know what else I can do.' Lord Ravenmere shrunk slowly back from the webcam as he spoke, shrinking in size as the chairman's eyes burned through the screen at him.

'I'll have a team in the air in the next couple of hours. You have until they get there to find something out,' growled the chairman, cutting the screen off before he had to listen to Lord Ravenmere's whining voice again.

The intercom buzzed, a thankful distraction from his annoyance at Lord Ravenmere.

'Yes, Sandy.'

'Your son is here, sir.'

'Send him in please,' he said swinging around in his chair to face the door.

It opened and a man walked in. He looked immaculate in a charcoal-grey tailored suit, polished shoes and a white Armani shirt with a silk tie. His face lacked any warm expression or greeting or emotion. He stood up straight, looking his father in the eye, waiting for the instruction he knew would come next.

'Your brother Tan is dead. He got careless,' the chairman said, unsure whether he'd get any reaction: a cry, a scream perhaps. None came. Lei's eyes narrowed and his jaw tensed at the news before his face sank back to its unreadable blank.

'How did he die?'

'Lei, the loss of your brother is not our prime objective. The organisation has been compromised and your mother's dream is under threat. I need you to put thoughts of your brother aside. Take care of this list in Europe—quick and clean—then you can join your brother and avenge your brother Tan's death.'

'How did he die?' insisted the Chinaman, his eyes cold and threatening as he looked at his father.

Unnerved and slightly afraid, the chairman answered, 'A British asset called Daniel Pearson. First the list, then the Englishman.' His words were cold, and he held Lei's stare. The Chinaman finally gave a nod of confirmation and left without saying a word.

Waiting for the door to click behind him, the chairman turned and looked at a photo on the cabinet in the corner. The woman at the centre with bright blue eyes and long blonde hair was his wife. They couldn't have children of their own, so to appease his wife's desperate longing, they had adopted three tiny Chinese babies. Triplets. The maternal joy was clear on her face as she held them proudly on her lap, swaddled in blankets. Their mother had died in childbirth and their father was too poor to look after them.

The chairman never felt the loving bond his wife displayed so clearly in the picture, but they made her happy which was all that mattered. The happiness was short-lived. She was struck down with cancer just after their ninth birthday. The chairman, with all his money and power as America's richest Texan oil tycoon, still couldn't save her. When she died he shut his emotions away. The boys grew up with nannies and home tutors. The chairman spared no expense. The boys excelled in all studies, taking a special interest in the martial arts and ancient combat techniques. Devoid of love and the outside stimulus of children and friends to play with, the three brothers formed an almost telepathic bond, rarely showing emotion or speaking. As they grew up and the chairman's plans grew, he realised how their talents and loyalty could be used to serve his needs.

His wife had been a prominent environmentalist, writing papers and attending seminars and campaigning all over the world. Consumed by grief and the injustice of her death, the chairman threw his money and power into a plan to provide power solutions with zero environmental impact of the planet. Over the next twenty years the board was born, it's influence and power growing and spreading across the globe. But as fast as he tried to make things better, power, greed and religion always separated continents with endless pollution and war and human suffering. That's when the board evolved, planning to change the world through force and manipulation.

The chairman was close to his goal: clean energy; clean water; the eradication of fossil fuels; most importantly, his controlling hand spread across the globe... all within reach. She would have been so proud. He couldn't let Haku's carelessness and this man Pearson screw it all up.

A tactical retreat today, come back stronger tomorrow.

The chairman tapped the keyboard again. The same connecting message appeared on the screen. This time they answered it in seconds.

'Mr Chairman.'

'General, is the team ready to go?'

'Yes sir, they're en route and will be in the air in 40 minutes,' said the general, direct and businesslike.

'Good, good. Regarding our conversation on damage

limitation, I am in agreement: regardless of whether Ravenmere and Davis contain the situation, I have set the wheels in motion. No ties, no loose ends. While the war rages on, we can reappoint the board and still achieve our goal,' said the chairman, his voice getting stronger as he convinced himself he was doing the right thing.

'I believe that is the best course of action, Mr Chairman. Plan for the worst, hope for the best.'

'Thank you, General.'

Once again the screen went dead, leaving the chairman alone with his thoughts.

CHAPTER 37

'Where are we going, Scott?' said Danny.

'Kingston. I've given him a ring, he's expecting us,' Scott said, being unusually evasive in sharing any information about his contact.

'Who is this guy?'

'His real name is Neville, but he only answers to Byte Lord. He's a tad odd, dear boy. It may be best if you let me do the talking,' said Scott still looking a little sheepish.

'Byte Lord, Jesus. What is he, twelve? What's so great about this guy?' said Danny, already disliking the guy in his usual technophobic way.

'He has a particular talent in retrieving data. All data: deleted, damaged, partial and shadow. He's developed AI to interpret and rebuild missing or damaged segments of data, with remarkable accuracy, to rebuild the original information. So try not to upset or shoot him before he's had a look at the hard drive.'

'Ok, ok, I'll try my best,' said Danny, holding his hands up and grinning. 'I don't know. You just happen to shoot the odd guy here or there and nobody ever lets you forget it.'

Kate laughed next to him, her face lighting up for the first time since their night in the hotel room in Norwich. He smiled back at her as she moved in and kissed him on the cheek.

'Ugh, get a room, you tarts,' said Scott finally returning to his usual banter.

The mood in the car continued to rise as the sun continued to set, leaving the world in a streetlight orange-yellow glow. Tom followed directions and turned into a little suburban street on the outskirts of Kingston upon Thames.

'Which one is it, Scott?' said Tom, scanning the rows of semi-detached Victorian townhouses.

'Over there on the left, the one with the white Transit on the drive.'

They looked at the scruffy old Ford Transit van with *Computer Repairs* written in cheap blocky signwriting. The front garden was overgrown and messy with a knackered fridge freezer sitting in the middle of it.

'Seriously, Scott, is this guy for real?' said Danny, looking doubtful.

'Don't judge a book by its cover, old man. Byte Lord likes to keep a low profile,' he said as they pulled up outside the property.

Scott, Danny, and Kate got out while Tom waited in the car. The curtain twitched in the front room as someone peeped out at the sound of the car doors shutting. Scott tapped on the door. After a few seconds the sound of clicks and rattles worked their way up the door as an inordinate amount of locks were undone.

'For fuck's sake,' muttered Danny impatiently.

'Daniel,' said Scott sharply to quiet him.

'Ok, ok.'

The door opened a crack before crunching to a halt on a security chain. A chubby, round, pasty face, lost in a mass of unkempt ginger hair and beard stared out at them through little round glasses. He said nothing for several awkward seconds, his eyes flicking nervously between Scott and Danny and Kate.

'You didn't say anything about them,' he said, nodding his head Danny's way.

'I apologise, but we have a mission for the Byte Lord, it's of global importance and only you can help us.'

The flattery did the trick and Neville's face lit up.

'The Byte Lord will grant you access, come in,' he said closing the door to take the chain off before opening it fully.

The hall was a mixture of bad taste 1970s brown, burnt orange and green wavy patterned wallpaper. It peeled at the edges as it dropped to a threadbare shit-brown carpet, all gloomily lit by a single bare sixty-watt bulb hanging from its pendant in the middle of the hall. Stacks of papers and computer magazines, and boxes of old computer hard drives, keyboards and monitors lined one side. They had to skirt sideways to follow Neville as he moved to a back room. Looking at all the crap, Danny's faith in Scott's contact was disappearing fast. He failed to see how anyone living in this shithole could bring anything to the table. It didn't even look like he could make enough money to pay the bills. They followed him into what origi-nally would have been the dining room. While Scott walked casually forward with Neville, Danny and Kate could only stand in the doorway and gawp.

The room was painted bright white and fitted out with

stainless steel base units that circled from one side of the room to the other. The anti-static rubber worktop that followed it was awash with PCs, laptops and hard drives all hooked up with a multitude of different coloured cables. Their outputs were displayed on the wall-mounted screens that surrounded them. On the far wall, the worktop had a gap underneath for Neville to use as a desk. Sitting in a modern white leather chair, Neville looked up at a bank of nine monitors mounted from the worktop to the ceiling above. Each monitor was running complex strings of numbers and analytics.

'Wow,' Danny said moving across the rubber anti-static flooring to where Scott and Neville stood.

'Touch nothing,' said Neville, shooting Danny a look of distrust.

Scott handed him the damaged hard drive which he turned over in his fingers before sliding one of the thin drawers open from the stainless steel unit below. An immaculately-placed row of tiny screwdrivers lay inside. After selecting the right one, Neville opened the drive up and inspected the damage.

'Can you do it, Neville?' said Danny impatiently.

'Did the ignorant one speak?' he said to Scott as though Danny didn't exist.

'Listen, Dick Lord, can you do it or not? Because right now you are a gnat's hair away from me breaking your legs,' growled Danny, his eyes flashing dangerously at Neville.

The Byte Lord shrunk back behind Scott in panic.

'Daniel. Do you mind going through to the kitchen with Kate while the Byte Lord and I attend to the problem at hand?'

Grudgingly, Danny moved out of the room with Kate in tow. Behind him he heard Neville say, 'Bloody great ape, that was rather uncalled for. It'll take me an hour or so to extract the information and recover as much of the damaged sectors as possible, then possibly another hour for the AI program to rebuild probable missing sectors.'

'Thank you, your talents are appreciated, as always.'

CHAPTER 38

Lord Ravenmere walked swiftly through the busy early evening London streets. Although it was a short journey from the House of Lords to his exclusive gentleman's club, his eyes darted nervously at passers-by. Things had gotten out of control. Not only was he worried about the incriminating information that was still out there, he'd lost favour with the chairman—and with the fate of Cheng Haku still fresh in his mind, it was not a position he wanted to be in for long. He climbed the steps and entered the foyer of the centuries-old club to be met by the concierge.

'Good evening, Lord Ravenmere, may I take your coat, sir?'

'Thank you, Albert,' said Hubert, already feeling more secure in familiar surroundings.

'Your guest is already here, sir, he's sitting in your usual booth in the Green Room,' said Albert handing the coat to a minion to be whisked away to the cloakroom.

Albert escorted Hubert through the oak-clad rooms, past the soft Chesterfield leather sofas and secretive, high-backed, leather booths where centuries of powerful men and politicians had made their deals and collaborations that made the country tick through the ages. Albert entered the Green Room and stood to one side to let Hubert sit down next to his guest.

'Your usual, sir?'

'Yes please, Albert.'

'And another for your guest?' said Albert gesturing his white gloved hand to Michael Davis.

'Er, yes. Thank you.'

'Will you gentlemen be dining with us tonight?'

Hubert looked at Davis, who nodded in agreement.

'Very good, sir, shall we say eight o'clock?' Albert said as another minion appeared with the drinks and then disappeared with the same silent smoothness he'd arrived with.

'Yes, thank you, Albert, that will be all,' said Hubert, waving Albert off in the manner of expected service rather than an appreciated one.

Hubert's eyes followed Albert until he was out of sight and earshot, then turned their focus front and centre on Davis.

'Michael, please tell me you have something,' he said sounding a little more desperate than he intended to.

'As a matter of fact I do. The hospital job was too organised, planned and clinical, too much like one of our jobs. So I've had men looking at internal irregularities. Turns out one of our own has been taking a big interest in some of our arrangements. It also turns out he's been away from his desk since the hospital job. The investigation stated in his log is completely bogus.' Davis spoke with a calm confidence that started to make Hubert feel more relaxed.

'Who is it, Michael?'

'One of my senior agents, Edward Jenkins. I pulled his file and it appears he's worked with Howard's boy, Daniel Pearson, and Howard's annoying ex-military intelligence buddy, Paul Greenwood.'

'Brilliant, what's the plan?' said Hubert, suddenly excited at the prospect of fixing the mess he was in and returning to favour with the chairman.

'I suggest we get the Chinaman and our remaining asset to scope out his house. He'll turn up there or at the office soon enough. We'll track him back to Pearson and the information, ready for the chairman's team of assets arriving from America,' said Michael, breaking off as Albert returned.

'Your table is ready, gentlemen, if you would like to come through.'

'If you could give us a couple of minutes, Albert, I just have to make a call,' said Hubert, pulling his phone out with his podgy little fingers.

'Certainly, sir,' said Albert stepping away to give them privacy.

'What's Jenkins' home address, Michael?'

Hubert dialled as Davis slipped a piece of paper across the table. It rang only once before being answered.

'Yes,' came the Chinaman's usual response.

'I have a lead for you. Edward Jenkins. He's an MI6 operative with connections to Daniel Pearson and Howard. We think he's the one behind the hospital conflict. I have his home address. Find him, follow him, and get the information back. Then kill them all,' said Hubert, the confident arrogance returning to his voice as he convinced himself he was back in control.

'The address,' came the Chinaman's response, short and direct.

WHO HOLDS THE POWER

Hubert relayed the address and hung up. He put the phone away before standing and gesturing for Davis to go first.

'Let's eat, shall we?' he said as Albert returned silently to escort them to the table.

CHAPTER 39

Glugging his third cup of coffee in the dated, sparse kitchen, Danny nosed inside the cupboards. Apart from tea, coffee, sugar and milk they were bare. The fridge was empty apart from an M&S salad bowl and a chocolate eclair.

Strange.

Scott wandered through, flicking the kettle on as he entered.

'How does that weirdo live in this dump?' Danny said to Scott in a low voice, not wanting to upset the Byte Lord before he'd finished his greatness.

'Oh, he doesn't live here. This was his mother's house. He just works from here. You're privileged, dear boy, very few people ever see his place of work. The Byte Lord likes his privacy you see. Data is a very desirable commodity and very lucrative, especially when that data doesn't technically belong to the person asking to retrieve it,' Scott said, raising his eyebrows and giving a knowing smile.

'He deals in industrial espionage then.'

'That, and secrets and client lists, all that kind of thing.

150

He's extremely good at it. He actually lives in a six-million-pound penthouse in Greenwich, overlooking the Thames.'

As Danny and Kate sat dumbfounded, the Byte Lord poked his head around the door.

'All finished,' he said nervously, pushing his little round glasses up his nose before disappearing back into the room.

They filed in behind him, noticing three of the screens were full of the notes and email files Scott had shown them in the hotel in Norwich.

'The screen on the left shows the intact files recovered from the hard drive; the screen in the middle is the damaged data files fixed by my AI program to an accuracy of 99% of the original file; the screen on the right shows 17 files damaged beyond total recovery.'

As Neaville went on enjoying displaying his own brilliance, a file caught Danny's eye on the right-hand screen: *Tipping.. oint Wedne... 19th J....*

'Hey, Gay Lord, open that file for me,' said Danny with a look that made Neville think twice about protesting.

He opened it up, displaying a report to the board from General Harley Buchanan. Large parts of the message were missing and some others unreadable but the opening sentence said enough: *Assassination of Cr... Prince Abdullah Bin Salm... Medina... sniper... official visit Wednesday 19th June.*

'Shit, that's tomorrow. Wrap it up, guys, we've got to get this back to Howard.'

Neville copied all the data to a new hard drive for them, complaining bitterly to Scott about the way Danny spoke to him. Within minutes of finishing, Danny had briefed Howard, and Tom was working his way through the night-time traffic back towards base.

They arrived to a hive of activity. Howard, Paul and Edward were all on phones, while scribbled notepads littered the dining table, and laptops sat open on maps of

Saudi Arabia and the streets of Medina. Howard indicated for them to sit while he talked. Scott instinctively pulled out his laptop, plugged it in and fired up the information on Neville's hard drive. Howard and Edward finished their calls and sat at the table while Paul continued talking.

'Ok, time's short and options are limited. If the board manages to assassinate the Crown Prince of Saudi Arabia, America will be incriminated and it will undoubtedly be the final catalyst between the two countries. War is certain to break out. If we alert the Saudis, it could still be construed as an American plot in retaliation for the embassy killings. If we alert The States about this on the basis of one partial email, one, they won't take it seriously, and two, the board will go to ground before we can find out who the chairman is. The best chance we have for stopping this is men on the ground: scope out sniper locations and intervene. I can get two men on a cargo plane bound for Badr tonight. I'd like you and Tom to go,' said Howard looking at Danny then at Tom before turning to look at Paul, who was still on the phone to the aviation freight company. He nodded and gave a thumbs up.

'Good. I've arranged for a guide to drive you from the airstrip to Medina. You should be able to get there before noon tomorrow, giving you a few hours before the official visit to find the sniper and stop him. It's tight, but it's all we have. I don't need to tell you if they succeed in killing Crown Prince Abdullah Bin Salman, you'll need to get out of there fast. The Saudis will go nuts; they're liable to shoot or behead anyone who looks like a Westerner, without question.' Howard finished and looked at Danny and Tom for an answer.

They both looked at each other, a knowing look that took them back to the days of service—Danny's in the

SAS, and Tom's as a corporal in the Paras. Turning back to Howard, they both spoke in unison.

'Weapons?'

'We can't get anything through security at the airport for the cargo plane. The guide will have handguns; no silencers I'm afraid. He also has native clothing for you. It's all I could arrange at short notice,' said Howard checking his laptop as he spoke.

'There are clothes and kit bags upstairs. They've got the prince's itinerary, maps and his route highlighted in them, radios and money for emergencies. If it all comes on top, try to bribe or buy your way out. That only leaves me to wish you good luck, gentlemen. One of the men will take you to the airport, you leave in fifteen minutes.'

With that, the meeting was over. Howard moved onto Scott and the information from the hard drive. Danny noticed Kate looking lost at the back of the room and went over.

'You ok?' he said, putting his arm round her shoulders.

'What am I supposed to do?'

'Stay here, Scott will look after you. This whole thing will be over soon, and you can go back to your life before all this nightmare began.'

'Not everything's been a nightmare,' she said putting her arms around him, her deep blue eyes looking up at him.

'Yeah, not everything,' he said kissing her on the forehead.

'I've got to get ready to go. Sit tight. I'll be back day after tomorrow.'

Danny peeled her reluctant arms away from him, then put his hand through her hair onto her neck. Cradling the back of her head, he kissed her on the lips. Danny reluctantly pulled away after a few seconds.

'I'll be back soon,' he said again, moving away to join Tom, his eyes glinting alert and his face hardening as he got his head in the game. Tom was already on it. Both living in the adrenaline buzz of an operation. The same feeling as their first mission, relived every time.

CHAPTER 40

Several miles away, Doug sat in a black Land Rover parked in the shadows thirty metres back from Edward Jenkins' Georgian townhouse. He muttered and complained to himself as he thumbed his way through his Facebook page to break the monotony. He glanced up as he'd done every few minutes in the hope Jenkins would come wandering up to his house. Instead, the Chinaman stood directly in front of the car staring at him, a ghostly expressionless nightmare like Jason from the *Friday the 13th* movies. Doug jumped out of his skin, dropping his phone in the process.

'Fuck, shit, fucking creepy oriental bastard,' he said out loud, his heart racing.

The Chinaman moved around and got in the passenger side. Sitting down, he shut the door and sat staring motionlessly through the front window.

'You need to concentrate,' he said without turning to look at him.

'Yeah, whatever, you scared the fucking shit out of me,'

Doug said, looking down and scrabbling around for his dropped phone.

'Got it,' he said, sitting back up to find the point of a thin six-inch blade millimetres from his eyeball.

'Concentrate,' said the Chinaman, now staring coldly at him.

Doug moved his hand ever so slowly under his jacket to get his gun.

I'm gonna fucking kill this bastard.

He tried to grab the grip and felt the rim of the empty shoulder holster instead.

The Chinaman held up his gun with his free hand and placed it on the dashboard. He whipped the knife away and stepped back out of the car.

'Concentrate,' he said again, shutting the door and vanishing into the night right in front of Doug's eyes.

'Jesus, that fucking freaky bastard gives me the creeps,' he said out loud trying to calm his breathing down. He picked his gun off the dash and slid it back in its shoulder holster, his hand shaking slightly as he did so. Slapping his cheeks, he sat, eyes glued to the road.

Concentrate, Dougie boy, concentrate.

A black Mercedes turned into the street just before midnight. The sudden brightness from its blue-white Xenon headlamps made Doug jump. He slid down low in his seat and clicked the talk button twice on his radio. It responded a second later with another two clicks. The car pulled up outside the house and a man in a suit got out. Doug watched the shadowy figure look up and down the street slowly, as if he suspected Doug was there. False alarm. He opened the little iron gate and walked up the path to his front door. After one last look behind him, the figure went inside.

Edward closed the door and locked it behind him. After tapping the alarm code into the keypad on the wall, he walked through to the kitchen. He filled a glass from the tap and turned his back to the window as he drank. Something made him freeze, glass to his lips. An atmosphere, a change in the ionisation in the air, or just plain sixth sense. He didn't know. He just had the feeling someone had been in his house. Pulling a little stubby pistol from his shoulder holster, he stood there listening. Was that a faint creak from deep within the house? Edward listened hard, until the sound of his own heart and the blood rushing in his ears overtook the silence. Treading lightly, Edward moved through the downstairs, sweeping the dining room, lounge and study. Nothing. No sounds. Everything looked to be in its normal place.

Relaxing a little, Edward made his way up the stairs. The eerie feeling of eyes boring into his back made him spin around fast at the top. Nothing but the night-time gloom of the ground floor stared back at him.

Pull yourself together, Ed, you're seeing ghosts.

The Chinaman slid behind the lounge door as Edward came in. He heard every soft step Edward made. There was no pounding heart or blood rushing in the ears for him. His father had made them study many forms of Chinese martial arts and also sent them to Japan to study Ninjutsu. His pulse rate didn't rise above seventy. As Edward moved out of the room to the stairs, the Chinaman followed in the blind, dead space behind him. His face was impassive, his movements so controlled they didn't even make his clothes rustle. He turned at the bottom of the stairs, just watching as Edward climbed them. Reading Edward's body language, he knew he was about to turn, and melted away into the hall a split second before.

He stood and listened to Edward moving about upstairs for a minute before heading silently for the front door. Picking up a takeaway leaflet from the table in the hall, the Chinaman opened the front door. Placing the leaflet between the Yale lock and the door frame, he pulled the door closed behind him, sliding the leaflet out slowly until the latch dropped silently into place without its usual loud clunk. The Chinaman left, walking confidently out through the front gate. He crossed to the car and tapped on the window.

'The tracker,' he said to Doug as he lowered the window.

Doug handed him a small black box slightly bigger than a cigarette packet. The Chinaman took it and moved to Edward's car. He bobbed down and pushed it up out of sight in the wheel arch, where it grabbed onto the body-work with magnetic attraction. Returning to the car, he got into the passenger seat next to Doug.

'We go. He's there for the night. We have the car tracked and three hidden cameras and mics in the house.'

Tired and fed up, Doug couldn't be bothered to answer. He pulled away smoothly, only turning the lights on once they were away from Edward's house. Ten minutes later the Chinaman felt the phone in his pocket buzz. He pulled it out and read the message.

Terminate Ravenmere and Davis.

CHAPTER 41

Dressed in beige combat trousers, desert boots and beige canvas jackets, Danny and Tom sat in the two rows of seats fitted behind the pilot's cabin, small galley kitchen and toilet. Everything behind them on the cargo plane was stripped out, all the way to the large loading bay door at the rear. The floor was comprised of metal gridwork with anchor points evenly spaced for strapping cargo down. In this case it was three vintage sports cars being delivered to Sheikh Almat El Molam, a rich Arab with his own landing strip just outside Badr, a two-hour drive from Medina. They studied the maps and the itinerary for the crown prince's visit, both coming up with the most likely locations for a sniper to take his shot.

'I agree, mate, when the target exits the new hospital and does the usual handshake, a few words, bollocks, blah, blah, the sniper will take him out,' said Tom, running his finger up the map.

'That's when I'd do it,' said Danny. 'There's three roads leading away from the square outside the hospital. Even without seeing it there's got to be numerous locations within a 1000-foot radius, especially with all the residential apartment blocks in the area. We've got multiple split-level towers and roof terraces he could choose,' Danny continued. He drew a triangle shape on the map, with the point on the prince's exit from the hospital, going forwards in a V to the flat top of the triangle that cut across the 1000-foot mark.

'Let's hope there are not too many options, considering there's only the two of us.'

'I say we start along the 1000-foot line. He's going to want to be close enough for a sure kill but far enough for a clean getaway,' said Danny catching two of the aircraft crew eyeing him curiously from the galley kitchen. It was noisy in the cavernous rear of the plane and they couldn't hear what he and Tom were talking about, plus they'd been paid a generous amount to ask no questions. All they had to do was deliver the cars to the sheikh and develop a mysterious plane fault for around ten hours, by which time their two passengers would be back and ready to fly home.

'What do you reckon our odds are of pulling this off?' said Tom.

'Hard to say without seeing it, probably 60/40 at best,' said Danny with a positive grin.

'Better than usual then,' Tom said joining in the pre-operational banter.

'Hell yeah, positively a dead cert, mate.'

As if on cue the plane started its slow decent, changing their mood instantly. Danny and Tom fell silent, checking their radios and satellite phone, stowing them with the intel into their rucksacks. The plane juddered and shook as it bumped down onto the rough tarmac. The two of them sat back, faces hard, concentrated and focused on the mission in hand as the plane taxied to a stop. The engines finally wound down and an amber warning light started spinning above the massive rear cargo door. It made a loud clunk as locks opened letting it lower slowly on its two huge hydraulic arms, eventually thudding down onto the tarmac to become the ramp for unloading.

Danny and Tom walked down the slope with the cargo crew. They squinted into the bright early morning sunshine, soaking up the blast of desert heat. Danny slid his sunglasses on before stepping onto the tarmac. They stood on their own for a while. The cargo crew wandered over to the sheikh's men, patiently waiting for the low-loader to arrive to transport the cars to the sheikh's estate. They took no notice of Danny or Tom as they looked around the airfield that sat alone in a huge expanse of nothing. Just a tarmac strip, a concrete pad, and a dirt track winding off to join the main road in the distance.

'What now?' said Tom, sliding his own wraparound shades on to kill the glare.

'Fucked if I know,' said Danny, searching the horizon for movement.

Five minutes later they spotted a tiny dust cloud approaching from the direction of the road. It grew slowly in size until they could see the bright reflection of sunlight off the windscreen of a car. It bounced and snaked along the dirt track until it got close enough to make out as a Toyota Land Cruiser. Hurtling onto the airstrip, the driver braked hard in front of them. The trailing dust cloud over-took him, obscuring Danny and Tom's view until it settled.

'Sirs, welcome, welcome. Come get in, we get the fucking hell out of here,' said a skinny Arab cheerily. He waved them over, his eyes wide and his mouth grinning ear to ear. Danny climbed in the front while Tom threw the rucksack in the back and jumped in.

'I'm Omar, bestest guide in all Saudi Arabia,' he said with his hand outstretched.

'I'm Danny, and that's Tom,' Danny said shaking his hand.

'Pleased to meet you, badass motherfuckers, let's go!' said Omar over-enthusiastically while screeching the Land Cruiser around and hurtling back down the dirt track.

'I've got your guns and some clothes for you. You can't go running around like that in Medina, you might get mistaken for Americans. Tensions are high. You will get your bloody heads blown off,' said Omar, grinning and laughing loudly.

'Thanks, I think,' Danny said, looking around at Tom while raising an eyebrow.

'Don't worry, Omar best guide. I look after you, no problem.'

'I feel better already,' said Tom sarcastically.

CHAPTER 42

Michael Davis left Number 10 Downing Street after a meeting with the Prime Minister. He'd been discussing the terrorism implications to the U.K. if war broke out in the Middle East. He walked past Big Ben and the Houses of Parliament and carried on over Westminster Bridge. He took the steps down on the other side of the bridge and started the fifteen-minute walk along the tree-lined, south-side embankment towards the MI6 headquarters, which was located next to Vauxhall Bridge. The picturesque footpath was full of office workers hurrying about, and tourists taking selfies and pictures of the iconic Houses of Parliament on the opposite side of the Thames.

While reading a message on his phone, Davis passed a suited man sitting on a bench reading a newspaper. Much to his annoyance the message was from Lord Ravenmere demanding he call him. Deciding to get it over with, Davis made the call. Ten feet behind him the only thing left of the man reading on the bench was a folded-up newspaper.

'Hubert, what did you w—'

A searing pain hit him in the back and moved through in paralysing agony to the centre of his chest. He felt the strength in his legs go as he dropped to his knees. Clutching his hands to his screaming chest, Davis gasped, his head spinning. All he could do was stare ahead of him, his eyes pleading for help. While tourists rushed over to help him he saw a suited man continuing along the embankment. The man turned his head when he was far enough away, only for a second, but long enough for Davis to recognise the Chinaman's expressionless face. Only then did it register in his mind: he was a dead man.

'Call an ambulance. I think he's having a heart attack.'

They lowered Davis gently to the ground, his phone dropping to his side. He lost consciousness as his skewered heart leaked its last beat. Horrified, Lord Ravenmere sat back in his office in the House of Lords. He pulled the phone away from his ear, his face drained of colour and his hands trembled.

Back on the south embankment, the Chinaman discreetly slid the ancient assassin's blade back into his jacket. It's eight-inch-long blade was only four millimetres wide and was as sharp as a razor blade. The Chinaman had expertly pushed it into Davis's back, his body masking it from view as he kept going. Easing the dagger forward through Davis's heart, he gave it a quick twist, tearing the valves before removing it and walking casually away down the path. The whole attack had taken only a few seconds.

CHAPTER 43

The huge C-17A Globemaster III transport plane landed at the United States Air Force base in Mildenhall, Suffolk, England. It rumbled towards the large blast proof hangers and pulled to a halt in front of an airman guiding it in by paddles. The large cargo door at the rear lowered as the propellers wound to a stop. A four-strong black ops team dressed in civvies—jeans, boots and black canvas jackets—walked out into the early morning chill. They carried large military kit bags on their backs as they made their way towards a uniformed officer and a waiting minibus. The officer saluted them and handed over a set of keys.

'Good evening, sir. The minibus is fuelled and ready to go. There is no record of your arrival on base, as per General Buchanan's orders. The guards at the gate are expecting you and will let you straight through,' he said with obvious pride at his efficiency.

'Thank you, Lieutenant, your co-operation has been duly noted,' said the lead. The other members of the team loaded the minibus and got in, blanking the lieutenant as if he didn't exist.

The leader got in the front, started the vehicle and headed for the front gate.

'What are you talking to that prick for, Hank?'

'Because, Kyle, that prick's going to get us back on base when we're done,' said Hank sarcastically.

'What have I told you about thinking?' came a deep, gruff voice from the back of the minibus.

'Yeah, yeah, McCormick. At least I went to school,' said Kyle, shooting a reply back at McCormick.

'Fuck you.'

'Ok, settle down. We've got a job to do,' said Hank just short of shouting. The minibus fell silent as he drove towards the armed guards at the gate to the base. The armed guards saw them approaching and raised the barrier. Hank drove straight through without so much as a glance in their direction. Following the sat nav on his phone he turned and headed towards the A11 and the way to London.

'What is this bullshit job, Hank?' said Lance from the back of the minibus.

'We're to retrieve stolen information that is of importance to national security. By any means necessary. The where and when will be provided by our contact in London.'

'Smells like bullshit to me, U.S. special ops on British soil without their knowledge or collaboration. This would normally be a phone call, a favour with the SAS or MI6 boys retrieving it for us,' said McCormick with murmurs of agreement from the lads.

'All right, pipe down. I agree it's odd but the orders are from General Harley Buchanan himself, so we shut up and get on with it,' said Hank dismissing them firmly. As he joined the motorway, he couldn't help feeling something was very wrong with this mission.

CHAPTER 44

I n Nairobi, Kenya, far away from the Ebola outbreak he'd unleashed in Sudan, Mambosa lay on a slatted wooden bench, relaxing in the sauna of the five-star Radisson Blu Hotel. He closed his eyes and put a towel over his face, soaking up the intense heat and steam from the hot stones on the oven in the corner. Just one more night before he disappeared down to Cape Town. He had his last payment from the board and he had the money he'd told the chairman the Sudanese president had taken from him. With false papers and a no-questions-asked flight on a light aircraft, Mambosa would soon be sitting by the pool in his newly-acquired six-bedroom house over-looking the sea in the sought-after area of Clifton, Cape Town.

'Did you feel anything for the people you sentenced to death with the Ebola virus?' said Lei in a soft, emotionless voice. The question was more of a statement than real curiosity.

Mambosa froze in terror at the sound of the China-man, caught between the urge to take the towel from his face and see, and the childhood instinct to keep his eyes covered—if you can't see them, they can't see you. He opted to remove the towel slowly. The Chinaman stood rigid and still by the door, next to the hot stones on top of the oven.

'The chairman wants to retire you from the board. Your services are no longer required,' he said, his lack of expression and movement adding an alarming amount of tension in the room.

'Money, I have money. Lots of money. I could pay you. You could say you killed me. After tomorrow no one will ever see me again. I'm getting out, a new name, new life,' said Mambosa, his voice getting higher and faster as he talked. As if the more words he got out, the better his chances of convincing the Chinaman to spare him.

'I think you and I both know that's not the way it goes.'

In some desperate hope of getting out and away, Mambosa leaped upright to charge the Chinaman. He barely got to his feet before the Chinaman moved at him in a blinding flow of speed and energy. He placed the palm of his hand on Mambosa's chest, only releasing his power in the last inch. To anyone watching, it would have looked as though he'd hit Mambosa with a 1000-volt electric shock. The blow sent him flying back, slamming into the wooden walls behind him.

'It would appear you've had a tragic accident, Mr Mambosa,' the Chinaman said, gripping him around the head and twisting his neck violently, snapping it and killing him instantly. Picking him up, the Chinaman dragged him towards the door and slammed his head down into the corner of the metal tray that held the heated stones, gashing Mambosa's temple deeply. Putting the towel by his feet to look like he'd tripped, the Chinaman stepped over

STEPHEN TAYLOR

the pool of blood spreading its sticky way across the sauna floor and left. Standing outside, he straightened his suit jacket and took a towel from the pile on the shelf. He dabbed the beads of perspiration off his forehead, folded the towel, and placed it neatly back into position. Turning away from reception and the exit, the Chinaman pushed the bar on a door and left by the fire exit, passing underneath the CCTV camera he'd disabled earlier.

CHAPTER 45

Dressed in traditional Saudi thobes and shemagh headdresses, Tom and Danny stood at the far end of the square outside the hospital in Medina. Positioned with their backs to the waiting crowd, press, police and the prince's personal security personnel, their eyes flicked and scanned the windows and rooftops from behind dark sunglasses as they mentally worked out distances and trajectories from each identified sniper location.

'How long have we got?' said Tom.

'Just over an hour.'

'Shit, let's hope the prince is late out.'

'How many do you make it?' said Danny never taking his eyes off the skyline.

'Five possibles, three probables' replied Tom, matter of fact.

'I agree. Five-storey red building on the left. Similar one behind the building site dead centre. The tall apartment off to the right. Gut feeling?'

'I'd have to say left or centre.'

171

'I'll go with that. Which one d'you wanna take?' said Danny with a grin.

'Left one.'

'Ok.'

Danny turned to Omar who had been watching the growing crowd.

'Omar, take the car up by that gas station. Wait there with the engine running. If this goes tits, we'll need to get out of here fast.'

'Ok, boss,' said Omar, immediately scooting off towards the car.

'Radio check, one, two,' said Danny moving away from Tom.

'Copy that. Check one, two.'

'Copy that, moving out,' said Danny splitting off from Tom, who disappeared out of sight up the left-hand road.

Walking briskly, but not fast enough to draw attention, Danny made his way past the windowless scaffolded shell of an apartment building next to his possible five-storey apartment block. He looked up towards the roof—not expecting to see anything, but you never knew—then moved to the entrance, pleased to see unlocked doors with no door entry system.

'Entering building now,' he said over the throat mic covered by the thobe.

'Copy that. Got a buzz lock. Wait. *Shukraan jazilaan* —thank you. I'm in, heading for the stairs now.'

'Copy that,' said Danny ploughing up the stairs floor by floor, only slowing as he approached the door to the roof.

He did a quick double check down the stairwell to figure out which side of the building the roof access opened out onto, then pushed the bar to open the door.

It didn't budge.

Danny backed up and shoulder-barged it. It still didn't budge.

'Can't get access to the roof. What about you?'

'I'm on the roof, it's all clear. Hang on, I'll climb on top of the plant room, see if I can see the rooftop of your building from here,' said Tom pulling himself up to the highest point.

'Anything?' said Danny, desperate for information.

'Wait. Er, your door's been wedged shut with a metal bar,' said Tom, squinting as he scanned the distant roof in the bright sunshine. 'No, I can't see any... Wait. I've got eyes on... Target's lying down. I can just see his boots behind the satellite dishes.'

'Shit, keep eyes on. How much time have we got?' said Danny as he hurtled down the stairs, jumping them flight at a time.

'Not long, four, five minutes at most,' said Tom, swinging to look from the rooftop to the hospital entrance and then back again.

Leaping the last flight into the foyer, Danny bounced off the wall with his shoulder and charged the entrance door, just managing to keep on his feet he blasted through the door and stumbled down the steps. Running next door, Danny jumped up and pulled himself over the fence surrounding the deserted building site.

'Where are you, Danny? I've got officials coming out of the hospital,' said Tom, the tension building in his voice.

'I'm coming up the building behind,' grunted Danny as he appeared out of the bare concrete staircase onto the roof. Pulling the gun from his thobe, he ran at full pelt towards the building next door.

'Fuck, hurry, Danny. The prince is stepping up to the podium,' Tom said, spinning back round to see Danny launch himself off the edge of the building site roof.

Danny leaped across the fifteen-foot gap between the two buildings. Landing in a forward roll, he used the momentum to roll up into a run before diving on the sniper as he fired. The barrel of the rifle twitched up a couple of millimetres as the high-velocity bullet exited. It hit high of its target, making a perfect hole in a first-floor storage cupboard window before embedding itself in the wall behind stacks of neatly folded bedsheets.

Dressed in similar local get-up to Danny, the sniper spun round onto his back. Elbowing Danny in the head as he turned, he grabbed Danny's gun hand by the wrist. To Danny's surprise, the sniper was Middle Eastern, wiry, and tough. He punched Danny hard in the throat, causing Danny to drop his gun as he threw him off to one side. Quick to his feet, the sniper took off, running towards the gap and the building site next door.

Danny moved after him, coughing as he drew air past his bruised Adam's apple. Knowing he wouldn't be able to catch the sniper, he grabbed the metal bar wedging the rooftop door shut. Gripping it with both hands, Danny swung it violently around. With his eyes locked on his target, he let its hefty weight go and watched it spin off towards the sniper.

The bar caught him in the base of his spine, just as he leaped to clear the gap between the buildings. The blow knocked him off-line, smacking him into the brickwork just below the roofline of the building site. He hung there by the fingertips for a second or two before one hand lost its grip, shortly followed by the other. Danny watched him vanish down the gap, followed by several sickening bangs and a thud as he bounced off an air-conditioning unit on the way down.

'Target's down. Get to the car now,' said Danny,

already dismantling the American McMillan TAC-338 sniper rifle and shoving it into its holdall.

'Copy that, already on my way.'

Danny slung the holdall over his back, picked his gun up and made his way down the stairs. He walked casually out the entrance door, circling away from the alley between the buildings with its shouts and screams as they discovered the sniper's body. Less than a minute later he climbed in the back of the Land Cruiser, sweat dripping down his face.

'Drive, Omar, let's get the fuck out of here.'

Ok, boss. I'm getting the fucking hell out of here,' said Omar, grinning from ear to ear.

CHAPTER 46

Doug sat on the battered old sofa in the disused warehouse. Boredom had set in and he was passing the time by throwing screwed-up takeout wrappers into a waste bin with varying success.

'Where the fuck are these bloody yanks? Yes!' shouted Doug as he got one in the bin.

Out of paper ammo, Doug got up and walked over to the bin. He bent down and reached in. Grabbing a handfull of paper balls he went to stand up straight. Without hearing anyone enter Doug froze as the muzzle of a rifle touched the back of his head. Dropping the balls, Doug spread his arms out wide with his palms up. He slowly straightened up to face three more rifles pointed at his head from in front.

'Whoa, boys, take it easy. You're the Americans, yeah? I've been waiting for you,' said Doug smiling and trying to look confident.

'I was told we'd be meeting a Chinaman,' said Hank, his rifle still at Doug's head.

'The Chinaman couldn't make it, so you've got me.

Ok. We've tracked the target to an address in Dulwich and we believe the stolen information is there with him,' said Doug, growing in confidence as Hank's team lowered their rifles. 'Fuck me, you guys are good. I never heard a thing.'

'Let's go, you can take us to the address then keep out of our way,' said Hank, ignoring Doug's chat.

'Ok, ok, I'll get my stuff,' said Doug, waiting for Hank to nod the ok for him to move.

'Bullshit mission, man,' said Lance shaking his head.

'Yeah, something ain't right, Hank,' said McCormick.

'Keep it down, guys. We go and assess the situation. If the job's rotten, I'll call it. Ok?' said Hank, eyeing his team one at a time.

He was their leader and had their respect and trust. They nodded their agreement and started to move out.

CHAPTER 47

That's the last of it, old boy. It's over to you now,' said Scott, bringing up the last piece of information.

'Thank you, Scott, absolute top job,' said Howard turning the laptop so Edward could see it.

Picking up a marker pen, Edward moved to the white-painted wall running down the far side of the dining room. He went to the right-hand side and wrote the information on the end of what was five metres of names, events, plans and places. Resembling a major incident room, the wall was criss-crossed with connection arrows, stick-it notes and printed out photos.

'Don't worry, my dear, once we get this out you'll be able to go home and get on with your life,' said Howard to Kate who was sitting quietly in the corner.

She smiled back at him then asked, 'When's Danny back?'

'Len and Phil will be heading off to pick them up from the airport in a minute,' said Edward nodding at the two serious-looking men sitting at the kitchen table.

'I'll go with them. I've got to get out of this place before I go stir crazy,' she said, springing out of her seat to join them.

'Ok, but straight there and straight back,' ordered Howard, moving his wheelchair around to return to the wall with Scott, Paul and Edward.

They checked and deliberated the information for a further half an hour until they couldn't take it any further.

'Right, what to do next. Now we've stopped the board's assassination attempt on the Crown Prince of Saudi, the immediate threat of all-out war is at least delayed. I could take all this to the Prime Minister and let him deal with America and the other countries. Alternatively, if we can get this information in front of the president, we could get General Harley Buchanan arrested, and he can lead them to the chairman, who I needn't remind you still remains anonymous,' said Howard.

'Who's the best person to get us in?' said Paul.

'I'm not sure. Perhaps we should ask one of these gentlemen behind us,' said Howard, turning with the rest of them to face two special ops soldiers, rifles locked and loaded. Seconds later two more swooped into the kitchen assuming the same position.

'All clear,' he said, training his rifle on Scott.

'I assume, as we're not lying on the ground in a pool of blood, that you're not going to kill us,' said Howard focusing his gaze squarely at Hank.

Hank didn't answer. Everyone remained perfectly still. The tension in the room grew thicker with every second. The only thing moving was Hank's eyes, flicking and scanning across the wall from left to right, landing on key words and names. The assassination of the crown prince. Embassy attack details before the attack happened, sanctioned by General Harley Buchanan. The board, the

179

chairman and their organisation spread across the globe. Hank only broke his concentration when Doug entered noisily into the kitchen.

'What the fuck are you all waiting for? Kill them and get the information so we can get the fuck out of here.'

'I'm calling it, boys,' said Hank, barely getting the words out of his mouth before McCormick, Kyle and Lance snapped their rifles around to line up on Doug.

'Drop the rifle, slow. Put your hands on your head and get on your knees,' barked Lance pulling some zip ties out of his tactical vest to secure Doug's hands and feet.

'Master Sergeant Hank Meadows, U.S. Delta Force,' said Hank, dropping his rifle in unison with his men.

'A pleasure to meet you, Master Sergeant. I'm Howard, British intelligence. This is Edward Jenkins, MI6 and Paul Greenwood, security expert. Lastly, Scott Miller, specialist computer services. May I ask, what is the purpose of your mission?'

'We are here under orders of General Harley Buchanan to terminate a terrorist cell and retrieve stolen government information,' he said, extending a hand to Howard.

'I'm guessing that's not your intention.'

'No, sir, it is not,' Hank said moving forward to study the wall.

McCormick moved next to him. 'What are you thinking, boss?'

'Is your brother John still on close protection detail?'

'Yep,' said McCormick checking his watch.

'I know, time's tight. If we leave now and divert the transport plane to Anacostia-Bolling, Washington D.C., we could be at the White House by 0800 hours, before the general has time to figure out where we've gone. If we get this wrong they'll throw us all in Leavenworth or have us shot. Anyone want to back out?' Hank said looking at his men.

'I'm in,' said McCormick, followed by Lance and Kyle.

'Ok, Howard, we'll help. But we need to move now.'

'We have a copy of the information here ready to go,' said Howard pointing to Scott who passed him a hard drive.

'Ok, can you take care of him?' Hank said pointing to Doug trussed up on the floor.

'We most certainly can. Here, take my contact details. Good luck, Hank,' said Howard, scribbling his number down.

'We'll call you when it's done,' said Hank, saluting Howard.

He turned, spun his finger to signal they were bugging out, and exited the house, leaving Howard, Paul, Scott and Edward all looking at each other a little shell-shocked.

'Well, that was rather intense, wasn't it?' said Scott, breaking the silence.

'You can say that again,' said Paul, noticing Edward looking at his phone messages and frowning. 'You ok, Edward?'

'Michael Davis is dead, killed by a long, thin blade inserted through the back and pushed through to his heart,' said Edward looking up from his phone.

'Where?' said Howard.

'South embankment, opposite the Houses of Parliament.'

'Any CCTV?'

'Blind spot, the camera's out of action,' said Edward unsurprised.

Finding a blank spot on the wall, Paul wrote Davis's name on it and drew an arrow down. He wrote another name, followed by a connecting arrow to Lord Hubert Ravenmere. Putting a question mark by it, he turned to the others.

'The Chinaman,' said Howard.

'They're cleaning house,' said Edward.

rgets,' the Chinaman responded with an equally unemo-
onal tone.

'What? Goddamnit. I've got to find out what's going
. You find Ravenmere and kill him. Once your brother is
ished in Europe, Ravenmere's the only one who can
d them back to me.'

'Yes, Father,' the Chinaman said, ending the call
hout further comment.

CHAPTER 48

The chairman sat in his boardroom watching
newsfeeds from around the world on the wall
monitors. He stabbed the keys on his keyboard as
he did internet searches for the assassination of Crown
Prince Abdullah Bin Salman. When it came up empty, he
tried the general's number again, as he'd done unsuccess-
fully every ten minutes for the last hour.

'Mr Chairman,' said the general's voice, direct and
controlled with an air of calmness.

'What the hell's going on, General? I'm hearing
nothing about Bin Salman's death,' said the chairman,
clearly annoyed.

'Mr Chairman, when planning tactical moves of this
magnitude there are no guarantees. We take our victories
where we can and our failures on the chin. In this instance
the crown prince is on his way back to Riyadh. I have had
no contact from my asset and can only assume the mission
has been compromised.'

'Goddamnit, just for once I'd like one damn person to

do a job properly,' shouted the chairman, failing to keep his anger and emotions in check.

'Hold your nerve, Mr Chairman. We may have had one setback, but we've also had one success. I've just heard that my men are on their way back from the U.K. Mission successful, enemy eliminated, and the information retrieved. They'll be Stateside in four hours.'

'I'm sorry, General, my outburst was unforgivable. That is great news. I can also confirm that our plans for a purge of the board are well under way. We must rebuild and plan for the future,' said the chairman, gaining his composure and control of the situation.

'Yes indeed. We must. War in the Middle East is still obtainable. The president is still on board. All we need is an alternative catalyst to tip the situation in our favour. I will reassess the situation. We will talk soon, Mr Chairman,' said the general, concluding the conversation.

'Yes, we will. Thank you, General.'

———

The Chinaman moved through Lord Ravenmere's Kensington home. There were clothes strewn on the bed and signs of a quick exit. He went into the lord's home office and searched through the drawers. He pocketed an address book and an itemised phone bill. He was about to leave when he spotted a note taped to the bottom of the drawer. Moving the collection of drawer junk out of the way, he read the password for Lord Ravenmere's computer. Flicking it on without hesitation the Chinaman logged in with the password. He checked the web history. He noted the search for train times to Brighton and checked the emails the lord had last read.

Hi Brian,

*Would it be ok to stay at the house for a few day
empty?*
Hubert

The reply was succinct.
Of course, Hubert, be my guest.

The Chinaman thumbed through the a
and found four Brians listed in its pages. He tu
computer and left the house as he found it. C
the Range Rover he headed back to the ware
he got there and found it empty, he tried t
Doug. The number rang until the answerph
Hanging up without leaving a message, t
climbed in the car once more. He drove
address Doug had taken the assets to, the
from the tracker on Edward's car.

The Chinaman parked in the shado
metres down the road from the house. I
dark he made his way to the house that
address. With nobody out on the d
Chinaman passed down the side of the bu
his way to the bottom of the garden. He
the high wall as if it wasn't there. Crouch
bery on the other side, he watched How
Paul through the large bi-folding doors
garden. Standing motionless, invisible
watched people enter the kitchen: mi
trained; Scott; the woman, Kate
followed by Daniel Pearson. He tens
Danny, assessing the situation. As good
take on those odds. Revenge for his br
wait. Leaving the way he came, he go
called his father.

'Yes,' said the chairman without f
'The team from America did

CHAPTER 49

After being woken up by the chairman with the news that his Delta team had not completed the mission as reported, the general rushed into his National Security Council office in the White House. Pulling rank and status, he wasted no time in waking half the command at Langley, ordering them to detain the Delta team as soon as they landed.

'What do you mean you don't know where they are?' shouted the general at Colonel Beauford Weiss, Vice Commander of Langley Airbase.

'Hang on, General.' As the colonel held the phone to his chest, the general could hear him barking orders at his staff. A few tenses minutes later he came back on the line.

'General, the transport changed its flight plan at the last minute and landed at Anacostia-Bolling, Washington D.C. at 0555.'

'Thank you, Colonel,' said the general hanging up without waiting for a reply.

He pressed the button for the White House operator. 'Get me the base commander for Anacostia-Bolling airbase please.' He hung up and waited, his mind racing as he tried to second-guess what the Delta team was up to. The phone rang within five minutes, breaking his train of thought as he grabbed it.

'Commanding officer Captain Rodriguez for you, General,' said the operator.

'Thank you,' he said as she connected him. 'Captain, I have a breach of national security. A Delta team landed at your base on diverted transport at 0555 this morning. I need them detained in isolation immediately.'

'I'm sorry, General, they landed, requisitioned transport and left an hour ago. Master Sergeant Hank Meadows had a signed authority order from yourself.'

'Not your fault, Captain. Do you have any idea where they went?'

'No, but the vehicle they requisitioned has a GPS tracker. Give me five minutes, General, I'll call you back,' said Rodriguez hanging up.

'Damn it,' said the general out loud. He drummed his fingers on the desk impatiently as he watched the minutes on the clock tick by infuriatingly slowly.

When it rang he snatched it up. 'Yes.'

'General, we've checked the vehicle. It's there at the White House, parked on the west side next to the Eisenhower Building.'

The general slammed the phone down, his face flushed with anger.

Those bastards are trying to warn the president.

'Sergeant,' he bellowed, leaping out of his seat and running out of his office. A surprised sergeant and three uniformed guards all snapped to attention. 'Come with me, we have a security breach in progress. We need to get to the president NOW.'

———

Hank and his team followed McCormick's brother, John, and three other of the president's close protection detail up the back stairs. They emerged in the corridor outside the president's executive residence.

'Hank come with me, the rest of you wait here,' said John opening the door to the residence.

Hank followed John along the hall towards sounds coming from the kitchen.

'Mr President,' John said loudly.

'John, you better have a damn good reason for bursting into my private quarters,' said the president in surprise, concern spreading across his face when he saw Hank in combats.

'I'm sorry, Mr President, but this is a matter of national security and treason. You have to see what's on this hard drive,' said John waving Hank forward, his hand extended to give the president the hard drive.

———

The general and the four guards charged up the main stairs with weapons drawn. They hurried along the corridor, running straight into the personal protection detail and McCormick, Lance and Kyle. Six guns snapped up in locked arms as both teams yelled at each other to drop their weapons and get down. Trigger fingers flexed and tension grew as the deadlock continued. Finally, the door to the president's executive residence flew open and John and Hank came out, guns drawn with the president positioned just behind them.

'Stand down, Sergeant, that's an order,' yelled the president at the guards in front of the general.

The order was immediately actioned as the men stood down.

'Gentlemen, place General Harley Buchanan under arrest,' he said, staring at the general in disgust.

'What I did, I did for America. I love my country,' said the general placing the barrel of his Beretta M9 under his chin as he pulled the trigger. The top of his head exploded in a plume of blood, brains and bone. With glazed, staring eyes he dropped to his knees before falling onto his front.

'Damn it,' said the president flinching away. He took a minute then pulled himself together.

'Thank you, Hank. We are indebted to you and your team. If you would like to go with John to the West Wing, once I've gathered the security council we'll call you in for a de-brief,' said the president shaking Hank's hand. 'Sergeant, secure the area and get someone to clean that piece of crap off my carpet.'

CHAPTER 50

Back at the house in Dulwich, the team sat around or paced up and down or drank tea and coffee. Anything to pass the time. They flicked through TV channels for breaking news, while Scott trawled the internet for any reports on White House dramas. When the clock hit 3:00 a.m. Howard's phone rang.

'Hello,' he said with apprehension.

'Am I speaking to Howard?' the voice said.

'Yes, you are, to whom am I speaking?'

'This is the President of the United States of America.'

'Mr President, it's a pleasure to speak to you,' said Howard putting his phone on speaker and sliding it into the middle of the table. All eyes in the room fell on the phone.

'The pleasure is all mine. I'm here with my security council and Master Sergeant Hank Meadows with his Delta team. May I ask for you and your team to formally identify yourselves?'

'In the room we have Edward Jenkins, MI6; Paul Greenwood, ex-intelligence officer; Scott Miller, computer

STEPHEN TAYLOR

security expert; and lastly, Daniel Pearson and Tomas Trent, special operations contractors. My code name is Howard. I head a special division of British intelligence that tackles threats to this country from foreign shores.'

'This is General Dale Parnell. Howard, I haven't had the pleasure of making your acquaintance, but I can vouch for the rest of these gentlemen. They were paramount in the obstruction and apprehension of Marcus Tenby and his plot to crash the financial institutions of this country. Not to mention saving the life of the U.K.'s prime minister and your predecessor, President Carter.'

'Thank you, General. I do remember reading the case file on that episode,' said the president.

'Mr President, may I ask what the news is on General Buchanan? Is he in custody and have you any insight into the identity of the chairman?' said Howard.

'I'm afraid not. The general took his own life before we could talk to him. We have experts looking into all his communications, but so far all we've found is Pentagon-grade encryption and untraceable IP destinations.'

'That's a shame. We have reason to believe the chairman is covering his tracks by killing off all members of the board that can lead back to him. We are currently trying to locate one of the members, Lord Hubert Ravenmere. I will contact our prime minister and brief him on events thus far,' said Howard.

'There's no need, the prime minister joined us on the conference call a few minutes ago,' said the president.

'Good evening, Howard. May I congratulate you and your team on an outstanding job. You have my authority to continue your investigation and detain Lord Ravenmere by any means necessary. Mr Jenkins, in light of Michael Davis's demise, I'm making you Acting Chief of the Secret Intelligence Service effective immediately. Please collaborate with the president's men and use the full resources of MI6 and MI5 to find out who the chairman is and the extent of the organisation.'

'Thank you, Prime Minister, I won't let you down,' said Edward a little taken aback.

'Gentlemen, it's been a long night and I have some delicate negotiations and the might of the U.S. military to stand down in the Middle East. It goes without saying, this matter remains strictly confidential. Good night and God bless.'

The line went dead, leaving the table tired and shell-shocked.

'Let's all get some rest, we'll start afresh in the morning,' said Howard turning his wheelchair from the table.

Jetlagged and yawning, Danny made his way upstairs. He stripped off quietly and slid into bed next to Kate as she slept. Rolling onto his side, he closed his eyes. Moments before sleep took him, Kate's arm moved around his middle, her fingers sliding through his chest hair. He could feel her breasts touching his back and soft kisses, hot and passionate, on his neck. Urges stirred from within as his tiredness took a back seat. He turned towards her and received a hot, passionate kiss on the mouth.

'I missed you,' she said, moving on top of him.

'Mmm, if this is what I get I'll have to go away more often.'

CHAPTER 51

igh in the Netherlands, north of Amsterdam, lie the West Frisian Islands. Located on the north shore of the central island, Ameland, and surrounded by a ten-foot fence topped with razor wire, lies WaveGen Corporation, a large wave and tidal power research facility owned by the board.

The Volvo 4x4 pulled up to the gate. Malcolm Janssen tapped his pass card on the pad and waited for the gates to open. He waved goodnight to the security guards through the CCTV camera on the fence and drove out on his 2-mile journey to one of the company houses in the island's largest town, Hollum. He yawned as he drove down the long dark private road from the facility. As he got close to the turning onto the main road the lights from the island's airport could be seen in the distance. The intermittent orange glare of a car's hazard lights blinking on and off lay ahead at the junction to the main road. When he was closer still, he could see the car had pulled to one side to get off the main road and was blocking his way past. He pulled to a halt. With his headlights on full beam he couldn't see anyone in the car.

Damn, I hope they haven't left it and gone off for help.

Malcolm got out and walked up to the broken-down car. He cupped his hands against the glass and looked inside. Nothing there. He tried the door to see if it was open, thinking he could roll it back enough to get through. It was locked. Cursing, Malcolm walked around the car and looked up and down the main road. Nothing. He looked back at the gap between the car and the ditch lining the road.

Maybe I could squeeze through.

He walked back to his car and decided he'd try to get past.

'Why did you join the board, Mr Janssen?' came a soft, calm voice from behind him.

Malcolm jumped out of his skin, his heart pounding in his chest as cold sweat ran down his back. He looked in the rear-view mirror to see the Chinaman's ghostly face lean forward, just enough to be illuminated every other second by the obstructing car's blinking hazards.

'What? I, erm, I wanted to change the world,' he stammered, scared and confused.

'The chairman wants to retire you. He thinks you have overstayed your usefulness,' said Lei unmoving, his eyes locked on Malcolm's in the mirror.

'That's ridiculous. I have achieved so much. I have so much left to do, the potential to help the world is enormous,' said Malcolm, part of his fear turning to anger and pride in his own achievements.

'That won't matter to the chairman, it's time for you to disappear.'

As the Chinaman's words sunk in, Malcolm froze to

STEPHEN TAYLOR

the spot, his eyes watching as the Chinaman's face sank back into the shadows.

A little while later the hazard lights turned off on the car in front, its engine started, and it drove off into the night. At the end of the private road, Malcolm's car sat with its engine ticking over and its lights burning endlessly into the night.

CHAPTER 52

The next morning the house was alive with people. Tom's team was packing up and Paul had gone to the office to check on Greenwood Security business. Edward left last night; as Acting Chief of the Secret Intelligence Service he'd set a manhunt for Lord Ravenmere in motion, hoping to find him and find out the identity of the chairman. Danny sat with Kate and Scott in the kitchen, the cabin-sized suitcases they'd bought in Prague by their feet.

'I'm off in a minute, can I give you two a lift?' said Scott checking the time.

'How's that then, Scott?' said Danny, puzzled.

'Oh, Edward had my car brought up first thing, no parking tickets or anything. Bloody marvellous.'

'That's great, mate. If you can drop us off at Kate's I'll check everything's ok then make my own way home,' said Danny looking at Kate who nodded her agreement.

It turned out Kate lived only two miles away from Danny in South Woodford. Waving Scott off he followed her inside the little terraced house and shut the door.

'Wait,' he said seeing clothes strewn around the living room and a mess in the kitchen. 'I'll check upstairs just to make sure nobody is still here. You check if anything's missing down here.'

'What are you talking about? Oh, no, no, I got in late from work the night I flew to Vienna. I had to rush like crazy to pack and get to the airport,' she said stopping him on the stairs and laughing.

'Ok, erm, do you want a hand tidying up?' he said feeling stupid.

'Are you sure? Don't you want to go home and get on with your life?' she said, her face falling and eyes searching for his answer.

'This is getting on with my life, if that's what you want as well?'

She answered by wrapping her arms around him and kissing him. When they eventually parted, she grabbed his hand and led him up the stairs.

'Let's tidy up later,' she said with a mischievous grin

CHAPTER 53

Tired and dishevelled, Lord Ravenmere peeped out through the gap in the curtains. The road looked as quiet as it had when he last looked, ten minutes ago. Satisfied, at least for the time being, he retreated in the gloom to his seat by the table. He rubbed his stubbly chin as he pondered his situation. Eventually he picked up the pay-as-you-go phone he'd bought yesterday. Holding a piece of paper up in the shaft of light streaming in through the curtains, Lord Ravenmere dialled a number with a shaky thumb.

'Roger, it's Hubert,' he said, forcing himself to sound as bolshy and condescending as he normally did.

'Christ, Hubert, what the hell are you thinking calling here? The police are looking for you and we've had MI6 agents in the House. They've packed up and taken everything from your office.'

'Shut up, Roger, my life is in danger and you're wittering on about the House of Lords' reputation,' Lord Ravenmere barked down the phone.

'I'm sorry, Hubert, I can't help you. I have a reputa-

66

STEPHEN TAYLOR

tion to consider,' said Roger speaking fast, dying to get off the phone.

'You listen to me, you little shit, I put you where you are now and I know all about you dirty little deals and backhanders. Not to mention what you did for the board. So be a good boy and do as you're bloody well told. I need you to find something out for me.'

There was a long silence. Lord Ravenmere's hand trembled as he contemplated the thought of Roger hanging up on him.

'What do you want?' Roger finally said.

'That's better. Now listen carefully.'

———

The Chinaman moved silently along the passage that ran down the side of Brian Wren's holiday home in Brighton. He tucked back behind the corner after spotting a neighbour pegging out her washing. When she'd gone back inside, he moved out and crept along the back wall, effortlessly walking crouched under the kitchen window. With his back flattened against the brickwork, he craned his neck and took a peek through the back door, taking in the kitchen. He couldn't see Lord Ravenmere, but there was a carrier bag full of shopping on the worktop and a coat thrown over the back of a chair around the kitchen table. Creeping the door handle down a millimetre at a time, it moved, unlocked and opened a crack. The Chinaman kept it there perfectly still, listening through the slither of a gap that opened into the kitchen. He could hear someone talking from the direction of the living room. Drawing a foot-long ornate dagger from a sheath sewn into the lining of his suit jacket, the Chinaman slid inside, closing the door soundlessly behind him.

200

Lord Ravenmere picked up the TV remote and turned it off. He couldn't stomach the news anymore. The reports of U.S. Navy and Army standing down in the Middle East after last-minute emergency negotiations between the president and the Saudi royal family were all over every channel. Tributes to General Harley Buchanan followed. The general died in the ambulance on the way to hospital after suffering a heart attack. He'd complained of chest pain shortly after the peace talks with the Saudi royal family and collapsed in his office at the White House. In local news, the head of MI6 and the secret services, Michael Davis, collapsed and died on the south embankment opposite the Houses of Parliament—the cause was not yet known. He sat in silence for a while, flinching at the sound of a floorboard creaking over near the kitchen. He turned around to face a figure in the doorway.

'I thought it would be you.'

'It's time to go.'

Four agents came into the room past Edward Jenkins. One handcuffed Lord Ravenmere and read him his rights. They lead him out the front of his friend's house in St John's Wood, London, and tucked him into a Range Rover with blacked-out windows.

'Take him to the safe house,' said Jenkins climbing into the car behind.

With another car in front the three moved off in convoy, leaving the area as fast as they had arrived.

———

The Chinaman moved to the living room. Seeing a man near the window with his back to him, he moved in closer.

When he was within a few feet and dagger raised to strike, the man shouted out.

'Sandra, did you bring the towels?'

'Yes, I've got them up here, Brian,' came a voice from upstairs.

'Ok, I'll take the boys down the beach before dinner,' Brian yelled back over the excited cheers from their two children somewhere upstairs.

In the kitchen, the back door closed with the faintest of clicks. Seconds later the Chinaman emerged at the front of the house and walked off casually down the road. He turned a corner and headed for his car. Before driving off, the Chinaman made a call.

'He wasn't there,' he said flatly.

'I know, there's been a development. Ravenmere's been in contact with Jenkins, the new head of MI6. He's trying to save his ass by doing a deal. Make your way back to London. Our contact is trying to find out what safe house they've taken him to.'

'Yes, Father.'

'Oh, and Yulan, I have the address of your brother's killer, just in case you want to pay him a visit.'

'Yes, Father,' said the Chinaman, starting the engine.

CHAPTER 54

The safe house was an unassuming three-bed terrace in Edgeware. It sat on a quiet road, with no cut-through for traffic, and tucked well away from the high street. Edward Jenkins nodded to the two agents stationed in a car outside as he made for the front door. Another agent inside opened it when he knocked. Two more agents sat at a small table in the living room while a tidier Lord Ravenmere sat on the sofa, shaved and showered and full of renewed arrogance.

'Well, have you sorted it yet?' he said, staring at Edward with disdain.

'Witness protection and new identities take time, as you well know, Lord Ravenmere. It would help if you gave us something in return. Like the identity of the chairman for instance,' said Edward trying to contain his annoyance.

'Oh no you don't. I get my deal set in stone, guaranteed by the prime minister. Then I'll tell you everything.'

'Then there's nothing more to talk about. I'll be back when I've spoken to the prime minister,' said Edward, pacing out of the room.

The agent at the door opened it for him as he approached.

'Thank you, Gavin. Keep your eyes open. You see anything suspicious, you call it in ok? The people after him don't mess about.'

'Yes, boss,' said Gavin, locking the door after he'd left.

Edward couldn't get an appointment with the PM and his security advisers until later that afternoon, so he made his way back to the MI6 headquarters by Vauxhall Bridge first. Swiping his access card, Edward entered the main office. On the far side one of his agents, Raymond Black, came out of Davis's old office. When he spotted Edward he looked unnerved for a second or two before shaking it off and approaching him.

'Hi, I was just looking for the file on the three men in Fulham we put on the terrorist watch list. The last time I saw it, it was in Davis's desk before you took the office over.'

'Eh, I think Margaret Sims was looking into that, Ray,' said Edward accepting his reasoning.

'Thanks, gov, I'll go and find her,' he said dismissing himself and disappearing towards the exit and lifts.

Sitting at his desk Edward signed into his computer. He answered a couple of emails and sat back in his chair. He had a thing about putting all the files and papers on his desk in neat exact piles, and now they were not. One file was poking out of the stack more than the others. Edward slid it out and opened it up. He stared at it then across the office, the cogs in his brain turning, putting two and two together. He picked up the phone on his desk and dialled an extension.

'Hi, Margaret, did Raymond Black come and see you about the Fulham guys?'

'Er, no. Why would he? He's had nothing to do with that case,' she said curiously.

'Sorry, my mistake. Thank you, Margaret.'

Edward put the phone down and looked at the file again.

'Shit,' he said out loud. Getting up and running out of the office, he left the file on the desk with *Lord Hubert Ravenmere* written on the front and the code name of the safe house on the piece of paper inside.

CHAPTER 55

A knock on the door alerted Gavin. He nodded to the two agents in the living room then went to answer it. The agents sat up and took notice but weren't unduly alarmed; it was probably the boss returning. Gavin followed protocol with one hand on his holstered gun, just in case. The black-suited figure looked distorted through the frosted window in the front door. It waved in acknowledgement as Gavin approached, making him relax a little. He placed one hand on the door latch and spoke loudly through the door.

'Who is—'

His words caught in his throat as a two-foot Han dynasty jian sword shot through the frosted glass, spearing Gavin just below his Adam's apple and only stopping when it chipped into the spine at the back of his neck. It retreated as fast as it appeared, leaving Gavin gurgling as his windpipe filled with blood. He dropped to the floor like a stone, paralysed from the neck down. The Chinaman's arm darted through the shattered glass and flicked the door latch up. Pulling his arm back out, he shoved the door with enormous power and speed. It slid Gavin's twitching body along the tiled floor enough for him to get in.

One of the agents from the living room swung into the hall, his gun drawn. The second he appeared, a perfectly balanced throwing knife launched by the Chinaman hit him with a thud in the centre of the forehead, flooring him instantly. Pulling Gavin's gun from his holster, the expressionless Chinaman charged down the hall. With an inhuman amount of skill and power he sprung off the left wall with one leg. The move threw him through the door opening. He dove into the middle of the living room with the gun extended and eyes locked on the last agent. Before the agent could move his gun to aim, the Chinaman had unloaded three bullets into his chest. Spaced only a centimetre apart they all hit his heart, killing him instantly. Flipping to his feet, the Chinaman stood, his cold eyes focusing on Lord Ravenmere.

'Wait, I've told them nothing. This can still work. I can come to America and work for your father, get a new identity,' said Lord Ravenmere rambling in a panic as sweat trickled nervously down his cheek.

'Your services are no longer required. Try to die with honour,' said the Chinaman, drawing the two-foot jian sword from inside his jacket.

'No, you can't. I won't. I'm a lord, goddamn you. I—'

The Chinaman powered the ultra-sharp antique blade across Lord Ravenmere's neck, sending his head rolling across the floor, an expression of shock and surprise locked on his face. Wiping the blood off on the sofa, he slid the blade away. The Chinaman made his way out into the hall, pulling the throwing knife out of the agent's head as he went. Wiping it and sliding it away, he continued to walk calmly out the front door and past the two agents in the car outside, whose shirts were crimson from their sliced necks and stab wounds made on his arrival.

Walking away as anyone would, he pulled his phone and made a call.

'It is done.'

'Good, the plane leaves in three hours. Avenge your brother and be on it,' said the chairman, his voice cold and hard.

'Yes, Father,' he replied to himself; the chairman had already hung up.

With a last look up and down the quiet street, the Chinaman saw nothing unusual. He got in his car and headed for Walthamstow.

CHAPTER 56

Finishing the conversation with Yulan on his drive in, the chairman moved through his offices giving out good mornings and friendly chit-chat. The staff were unusually jovial due to the chaos around the office—all the computers and company servers were being changed. The chairman had announced exciting new computer systems to take the company into the future. In truth he was having all the PCs and servers destroyed as an extra precaution. With the might of the Pentagon and FBI looking for the board and its chairman, complacency was not an option.

'Morning, Sandy, have the engineers finished in the boardroom yet?' he asked smiling pleasantly.

'Morning, sir, they have for a while. They have removed the conference equipment as requested. They said they would be back in the morning to install the new system.'

'Thank you, Sandy. I'm going to use it while it's quiet to make some calls. I don't want to be disturbed.'

'Yes, sir, I'll make sure you're not,' Sandy said, smiling and efficient as always.

He entered the boardroom, his face falling with the stress of the last few weeks. Pulling his new encrypted phone out of his pocket, he sat down amongst the spaghetti of cables left by the disconnected equipment and called Lei.

'Lei, where are you? Have you dealt with Janssen yet?'

'Yes, Father. I only have one more name to visit.'

'Good, very good. Call me as soon as it's done,' the chairman said sitting back and breathing a sigh of relief. His bravado returned as he started to think of his plans for the future. He would rebuild the board like a phoenix from the ashes. Bigger, stronger, he would control the world and go down in history as the visionary who saved the planet. His good mood was short-lived when a thought crossed his mind. The boys, his adopted sons. They were the weak link. Eventually some CCTV or the FBI or MI6 or Interpol would find a connection and tie them to a murder or disappearance. And that would lead them back to him. They would have to go.

CHAPTER 57

After spending the morning at Kate's, the two of them got a cab to Danny's house in Walthamstow. He showered and finally got a well-needed change of clothes while Kate made herself at home downstairs.

'Kate, are you hungry?' Danny shouted down the stairs.

'Yeah, but there's nothing in the fridge other than gone off milk and something with blue furry bits growing out of it,' she started shouting back until she noticed he was standing behind her.

He put his arms around her and kissed her on the neck.

'What do you fancy? Other than me,' he said with a grin.

'Mmm, aren't we sure of ourselves,' she said, smiling back.

'Yeah, what with my looks?' he said, pulling a goofy face.

She laughed and turned around to face him. 'How about pizza and a bottle of wine?'

'You can have the wine. I'll get some beers, there's an off licence next to Domino's on the high street,' he said, grabbing his wallet and phone.

'You go, I'll stay here and clean out this bio-hazard disguised as a fridge.'

'If you must. A woman's gotta do what a woman's gotta do,' Danny chuckled on his way out. Kate smacked his backside as he went.

'I'm going to walk. You can never find anywhere to park on the high street. I'll be about half an hour,' he shouted from the door.

'Ok,' she shouted back.

Kate gave the kitchen a clean down. It wasn't terrible, just showing the signs of no one being around for a while. She looked at the fridge and ducked under the sink looking for bin bags. When she didn't find any she searched through the cupboards until she found some in the cupboard under the stairs.

'Right, the fridge,' she said to herself.

She threw the blue furry thing out and all the other out of date bits tucked into the door. Wiping down the shelves she breathed a satisfied sigh. Kate closed the fridge door and jumped at the sight of the Chinaman standing behind it, his legs slightly bent, and daggers held in his raised fists. His face was a blank mask but his eyes stared with burning hatred. Kate wrenched the fridge door back at him and ran as fast as she could for the front door, dragging kitchen chairs over behind her as she went, in an attempt to slow him down. The Chinaman smashed the fridge door shut with his elbow, putting a massive crease in its front. He leaped over the chairs as if they didn't exist, his eyes never leaving their target. Kate got to the front door, only managing to get it open it a crack, before the Chinaman turned the blade inwards and powered his fist into her temple. The blow had so much power it threw her head hard into the wall opposite. She slid down to the floor unconscious as the Chinaman pushed the front door closed.

———

Danny paid the sales assistant in the off licence and carried the four-pack of beers and wine out of the shop. His phone went off before he reached the pizza place. Smiling at Kate's number on the screen he answered.

'You missing me already?'

'An eye for an eye, Mr Pearson. Time to pay for my brother's death.' The voice was cold and calm, but its sincerity couldn't be mistaken.

A split-second after the Chinaman hung up, the wine bottle smashed on the floor as Danny exploded into a run, his legs pumping and heart pounding. The mile and a half to the house seemed to take an eternity as his mind raced through unwanted scenarios. Running at the front door, Danny nearly kicked it off its hinges as he barrelled into the house. He grabbed the baseball bat he kept in the umbrella stand as he passed through the hall, wielding it as he entered the kitchen. His heart sank as he saw the chairs in disarray and the dent in the fridge door. Without delay he moved into the lounge, following it back round to the hall. With no one there he leaped up the stairs and kicked the bedroom door open, the sight in front of him freezing him to the spot.

Kate was in a kneeling position at the end of the bed, her hands tied wide to the bedposts, her head hanging down, obscured from view by her long blonde hair. The Chinaman had nicked the carotid artery in her neck with surgical precision, its cut causing a jet of blood to cover the floor and spray up the wall until her blood pressure dropped. At that point, Kate lost consciousness and died. Danny untied her hands and held her in his arms. He stayed there for a long time before laying her gently on the bed. His eyes narrowed and his face contorted. His entire body took on a granite hardness as he got Howard's card from his wallet. He rang the number on the *Oxford Financial Consultants* card.

'Oxford Financial Consultants, how may I help you?' said a cheery woman's voice.

'I need to make an appointment,' said Danny, his voice deep and gravelly.

'Will you be available on this number, Mr Pearson?' came a more serious reply.

'Yes,' said Danny, not knowing or caring how she knew who he was.

'You will be contacted shortly,' came the response before the line went dead.

Anger built to fury inside him only finding small release as Danny punched a hole through the wardrobe door. As he stood breathing heavily the phone rang.

'Daniel, what can I do for you?' came Howard's voice.

'He killed Kate. The Chinaman. He killed Kate in my house.'

'I see, are you all right?'

'I want you to find him. Find him so I can kill him,' said Danny in a low growl.

'That's a distinct possibility. Stay there. A crew is on its way.'

Howard hung up, leaving Danny alone. He turned with his back to the wall and slid down to the floor, a tear trickling down his cheek.

CHAPTER 58

Two cars and a black plain-panel van turned up at Danny's within half an hour. Two suited guys helped Howard out of the lead car and into his wheelchair. Tom joined him from the rear car as he wheeled his way up the front path. Four guys in paper overalls with arms full of cleaning gear and a discreetly-folded body bag got out of the van and followed closely behind them. Tom went in ahead of Howard, sweeping the ground floor swiftly as he went, moving in a circle back round to Howard at the front door, before moving up the stairs with his gun drawn in front of him. He smelled the iron odour of blood before he saw Kate on the bed and the arterial spray across the floor and wall. Danny was still sitting on the floor, his arms resting on his knees and his head slightly down as he stared at the pool of blood on the carpet.

'He killed her, Tom, the Chinaman just killed her like she was nothing,' he said in a resigned murmur.

'I know, mate, come on. Come downstairs and let the

215

lads look after her,' said Tom squatting down next to him as he spoke softly.

'I'm going to find him. I'm going to find him and fuck him up. I'm going to fuck him up really bad, and then I'm going to kill him slowly and painfully.'

Danny's face was hard and set, and his teeth were gritted in an inner turmoil between grief and fury.

'I know, mate. Come on, that's for tomorrow. Today let's sort Kate out.' Tom helped Danny up. He took a last look at Kate, then turned and walked downstairs into the kitchen.

Howard's men had straightened the kitchen up. They moved quietly past Danny as he came in. Picking up their equipment they went upstairs and disappeared into the bedroom. Slumping into a kitchen chair, Danny leveled his eyes on Howard.

'I've gotta get him, Howard. Let me see Ravenmere, I'll make him talk.'

'There's nothing I'd like more, dear boy, but the Chinaman got there first. The clean-up squad's over there now with five dead agents and a decapitated lord,' said Howard holding Danny's eye contact as the room went uneasily silent.

It was broken a few moments later by Tom entering the room with his phone glued to his ear.

'Yes, got it, I'll tell him,' he said finishing and turning to Howard. 'Edward's got the guy who leaked the safe house to the Chinaman. Bastard's an MI6 agent called Raymond Black.'

'Where is he?' growled Danny standing up, his face darkening with menace.

'Danny, mate, I don't think you're in the right frame of mind for this,' said Tom, trying to calm him.

'No, that's ok. I think a visit from Danny might be just

216

what it needs. Drive him over to headquarters, Tom. I'll let Edward know you're on your way.'

'Ok, do you want to change first?' Tom asked, looking at Danny's blood-stained clothes.

'No,' was all he said in reply.

Howard already had his phone to his ear as they moved to the hall. They had to stop as the men from upstairs carried Kate's body down the stairs and out the door, sealed in a thick black body bag. Tom wanted to say something but what was there to say? Danny didn't react. His emotions were buried down deep: grief replaced by a burning desire for justice and revenge. The men put Kate gently in the van and returned to clean up the room. Danny climbed into the passenger side of the car as Tom drove them off towards central London and MI6 headquarters. After ten minutes of silence Danny finally spoke.

'Thanks, Tom,' he said quietly.

It's ok, I'm there for you, mate.'

CHAPTER 59

Edward met them in reception, and despite the strange looks from reception and security, they signed Danny in and followed Edward towards the interview rooms.

'Danny, take it easy in there. I just want him unnerved enough to loosen his tongue, ok?' said Edward outside the room.

Without answering, Danny gave him a sideways look and a small nod.

Taking that as the best he was going to get, Edward opened the door and they entered the small, beige-painted interview room. Raymond sat on one side of a bolted-down steel table, on a bolted-down steel chair. He looked worried, with his arms folded and his knee bouncing nervously up and down. He shrank back into the chair as far as he could go at the sight of Danny pacing towards him, face like granite and eyes boring down at him, his fists clenched tight by his blood-stained side.

'Edward, what the fuck is this?' yelled Raymond, his eyes wide.

'This is just a little chat, Raymond. Mr Pearson here is an interested party. Very interested as it happens, especially as your friend the Chinaman has just killed his girlfriend after he'd killed five of my agents and Lord Ravenmere,' said Edward calmly, letting the reason for Danny's presence work on Raymond's mind. 'The problem I have, Raymond, is what to do with the treacherous little bastard who told him where the safe house was. Oh, and where Mr Pearson's house was.' Edward went quiet, sitting back and folding his arms, with Danny staring menacingly beside him.

'This is ridiculous, Edward. I haven't done anything wrong,' said Raymond, his eyes shifting from Edward to Danny and back again.

'You worked under the late Mr Davis, didn't you? Did you tell the Chinaman where he'd be the day he killed him?'

Edward's question seemed to throw Raymond. The colour drained out of his face.

'I want to see a solicitor,' he said, clamming up.

'Would you leave us, Edward?' said Danny in a low growl, leaning forwards towards Raymond.

Without answering, Edward stood and backed towards the door.

'No, what? You can't go. I want to see my solicitor, Edward,' Raymond said, standing as Edward opened the door and left.

'Do you know who I am, Mr Black?' said Danny, rising out of his seat slowly.

Raymond nodded as he moved behind the bolted-down chair trying to get as many things between him and Danny as possible.

'Good, then that'll speed things up a bit. During my training, the British government spent an enormous amount of time and resources teaching me how to interrogate efficiently, how to inflict pain, maim and torture people in order to get information out of them,' Danny said walking slowly around the table.

'Edward, anybody? Help!' Raymond shrieked before losing it and running for the door, banging on it. 'Help, Edward, I'll tell you everything, just get this lunatic away from me!'

The door opened and Edward stepped in. This time his face was deadly serious. He just pointed to the chair and said, 'Sit.'

Raymond quickly did as he was told and went to the chair, taking the opposite side of the desk to Danny who was walking towards the door. As he passed Edward he gave him a wink and left the room, joining Tom outside. They went to a small canteen down the hall while Edward finished the interview.

'I just want you to know, when we find him I'm in,' said Tom after they sat down.

Danny was going to argue with Tom about it, but he was too tired and emotionally drained, so he just nodded.

An hour later Edward put his head around the door. 'Let's go to my office,' he said.

When they were in and the door shut, Edward sat behind his desk and opened his notes.

'Ok, Raymond Black doesn't know who the chairman is and has never met the Chinaman in person. Michael Davis selected him when he found out Raymond's wife had left because of his gambling debts. Davis offered him a way out of his debt if he did certain favours for an associate of his. When Davis was killed, the associate contacted Raymond, offering him fifty thousand for the location of Lord Ravenmere and Daniel Pearson's address.

Raymond swears blind he had no idea what they were going to do next.'

'Ok, but how does that help us find the chairman or the Chinaman?' said Danny, the frustration clear on his face.

'I'm coming to that. The payments to Raymond Black came from a bank in The Bahamas. He got his money and instruction from a contact called Mr Pozo. We've traced Raymond's call records and one in particular sticks out: a VOIP internet phone with the IP address and number registered to—you've guessed it—FirstCaribbean International Bank in Freeport, Grand Bahama Island. As you know, The Bahamas is heavily used by U.S. companies for laundering, hiding money and tax evasion.'

'When do we go?' said Danny bluntly.

'Hold your horses, this is beyond my authorisation. Let me talk to Howard, he's the one who can get this kind of off-the-books mission cleared.'

'I'm going with or without yours or Howard's say so,' said Danny with a look not to be argued with.

'The same goes for me,' said Tom.

'Ok, guys, I know how you feel. Just give me a chance to sort it. Doing this with our help will be much better than without it. Look, Tom will take you home. Get cleaned up and get some rest. I'll contact you as soon as I can,' said Edward closing his notes and sitting back, waiting for Danny's agreement.

'Ok, tomorrow morning, latest,' Danny said.

CHAPTER 60

The road outside Danny's house had returned to its usual suburban quiet when Tom pulled up outside. Danny opened the door for them to go inside. He stopped in the hall listening to the silence of the house, a little piece of him hoping Kate would run down the stairs to greet him. Tom hung back, giving him his space as he walked through to the kitchen. Howard's boys had done their stuff. It was over-tidy, sterile. A new fridge stood in place of the old one, plugged in, fresh milk in the door. He walked through the tidied living room, delaying the inevitable. When he came back to the stairs, he turned to Tom.

'Make yourself at home, mate, make a brew, there's milk in the fridge. I just need a minute.'

Tom left him climbing the stairs. He paused outside the bedroom, eventually forcing himself to go in. It was clean and tidy with fresh bed linen and a new carpet underfoot. In his mind's eye all he could see was Kate's dead body tied to the end of the bed, kneeling in a sea of blood. Shaking it off he looked at himself in the mirror, shocked at the blood-stained, heartbroken image staring back at him. After a few minutes he pulled himself together, stripped and showered and went downstairs.

'I made you a brew,' said Tom, sitting on the sofa.

'Cheers, mate. You don't have to stay, you know.'

'I know, but I'm going to anyway,' Tom said, raising a mug to him.

'In that case we better get some beers and a takeaway in,' said Danny forcing a smile.

———

Danny woke with a fuzzy head. They'd had an Indian takeaway followed by a considerable quantity of beers and half a bottle of whisky. Eventually Danny drunk enough to push the nightmares of old out of his head so he could sleep. Venturing downstairs, he could hear Tom talking to someone in the kitchen. Scratching his unruly dark mop of hair, he walked in to see Howard in his wheelchair with one of his men sitting at the kitchen table as Tom fixed them all a brew.

'Good Morning, Daniel,' said Howard.

'Mmm, the jury's still out on that,' he said picking up the mug Tom put in front of him.

'Well, I think you may change your mind when give you these,' said Howard pulling an envelope out of his pocket and passing it across the table.

Danny picked it up and opened it, turning the two first-class tickets to The Bahamas over in his fingers.

'The British government and the President of the United States are extremely grateful for your assistance in this matter so far. They have given you their blessing to follow the lead to find Mr Pozo and see where it goes,' said Howard clicking his fingers to his man to place a briefcase on the table. Opening it, Howard pulled out a file, an envelope, and two mobile phones and slid them across the table.

'There is one condition. As an interested party, the Americans are sending two of their guys to meet you,' Howard said holding his hand up to silence them. 'Before you start, after some heated discussion an agreement was reached that Danny will be team leader. As you know, The Bahamas doesn't fall under British or American jurisdiction. You break the law and get caught and you're on your own, ok?'

'No change there then,' said Danny already flicking through the file with all the information they had. He looked up after a few seconds and looked Howard straight in the eye. 'Thanks for this,' he said.

'Keep me informed. There's money for expenses in the envelope,' Howard said signalling for his man to wheel him back to the car. He stopped at the kitchen door and turned back. 'If you find the Chinaman, I would appreciate it if you find out who the chairman is before you kill him,' he said, waiting for confirmation from Danny who responded with a small nod.

CHAPTER 61

Are you all right, Ian?' said Mrs McClusky to her husband.

Ian McClusky sat at the breakfast table, a cup of coffee on one side and a bottle of Pepto-Bismol on the other. He looked tired with dark rings under his eyes. Holding his belly as acid reflux rose higher up his throat, Ian unscrewed the lid of Pepto and gulped the pink liquid down. 'Sorry love, my stomach is killing me,' he said.

'It's that bloody place you work at. They put too much pressure on you.'

'I know, I know. As soon as things quiet down at work, we'll take a vacation. Jamaica or perhaps Mexico. We could go back to that hotel we had our honeymoon in. Would you like that?' said Ian, pulling his suit jacket on as he got ready to leave.

'Oh, that would be wonderful. I still think you should see a doctor about your stomach.'

'Yeah, yeah. I know,' he said, kissing her on the cheek as he made to leave. 'Pick some brochures up from the travel agent if you like,' he added smiling.

His face dropped as soon as he closed the front door behind him. Getting in his car, he backed it off the drive of his six-bedroom house in Fremont and drove away, heading for work at ECB in Silicon Valley. He decided to take Nimitz Freeway instead of Route 84 over Dumbarton Bridge. The traffic over the bridge was dreadful yesterday. His stomach acid complained again as thought about work. The chairman had been acting strange in their last communication, vague and reserved when Ian mentioned he couldn't get hold of Malcolm Janssen or Karl Lemitov. In fact, he hadn't heard from any of the board members in the last week.

Perhaps I should take that holiday and just get away, far away.

Half an hour later he pulled into his parking space in front of the large metal and glass ECB Power building in Silicon Valley. He said good morning to the receptionist as he swiped his pass card to enter the main building. He took another swig of Pepto-Bismol as he walked up the stairs, which made him feel slightly better as he entered his office and sat down wiping sweat beads off his forehead.

Sandra's right, I should see a doctor.

While he was thumbing through his address book for the doctor's surgery, his secretary popped her head round his door.

'Morning, Mr McClusky. I had a note from Wesley Mason on my desk. He would like to see you in the R&D department as soon as possible.'

'Thank you, Lorna. I thought Wesley and Andrew were still in Germany with VW and Mercedes.'

Lorna just looked at him blankly and shrugged.

'Ok, I'll go down there now,' he said getting out of his chair.

The research and development department of the vast ECB building was tucked in the rear corner. It was usually pretty quiet as only a handful of people had access permission to enter through its heavy steel doors.

'Are you down here, Wesley?' he shouted over the whine of the test bed machinery. The tubular framed mock electric car sat on a rolling road with a fat loom of cables attached to ECB's prototype high-output batteries. It simulated a wide spectrum of driving conditions while the monitors spewed out reams of performance data on the batteries.

Where the hell is everyone?

'Wesley,' he shouted again. Looking through the glass window in the lab doors he got a glimpse of someone behind the equipment at the rear and pushed the heavy door to enter. Ian headed towards the back looking around, only to find it deserted.

'Hel—' he started to say, turning back towards the door.

Standing stock still behind him was the Chinaman, staring intensely with an unreadable expression. Ian backed into a desk, knocking a stack of instruments over. He'd heard the rumours about the Chinaman and now he was here in front of him. Fear gripped his heart.

'Tell me, Mr McClusky, why did you start this business?' Lei said calmly, his expression never changing.

'What, erm, I wanted to make a change. Drive the world forward with clean energy,' Ian said, both puzzled and terrified in the same breath.

'The chairman wants you removed from the board.'

A few minutes later, while the security guard was outside dealing with a deafening car alarm, The Chinaman rewound and deleted the building's CCTV cameras. He turned the unit off before leaving the security office and walked out the front doors into the hot Californian sun.

CHAPTER 62

A puff of smoke came off the tyres of the British Airways Dreamliner as it touched down in the Caribbean sunshine of Grand Bahama International Airport. Danny and Tom worked their way through the sunny yellow-painted arrivals hall, both sliding on shades as they stepped outside. Danny dealt with Kate's death the only way he knew how to: he buried his emotions down deep and concentrated on getting justice for her. The two of them left the building and headed with the crowds of holidaymakers for the taxi rank next to all the tour operator coaches. The hairs on the back of Danny's neck stood up. He sensed or had seen something in his peripheral vision. Someone or more than one person out of place following purposefully, stealthily closing in on him.

'Heads up, incoming,' Danny whispered to Tom, his head straight ahead towards the taxis.

'How many?' Tom said in return.

'I think two about five metres back. You break left and I'll break right, confront them while we're in public. On three.'

'Ok. One, two, three.'

They split and turned fast, dropping their backpacks in unison. Tom faced up to his man, his feet slightly apart, weight balanced ready for action. The guy opposite him showed only a split second of shock before adopting a similar stance to Tom. Danny spun with lightning speed, grabbing his follower's jacket and drawing his other fist back ready to punch him out. To Danny's surprise, he countered the move with equal speed. As Danny's arm was swiped away, the man moved in to grab his jacket. Returning the counter, Danny moved away and stepped back out of reach. The man opposite moved back himself and smiled.

'Daniel Pearson, you don't disappoint,' he said with a regimented American accent.

'The Americans,' Danny said without returning the smile.

'Hank Meadows and Lance Swain at your service,' said Hank extending a friendly hand.

Taking the offering Danny shook his hand, followed by Lance's.

'You could have just held up a name card in arrivals, you know,' said Danny starting to relax a little.

'Where's the fun in that? Come on, let's go. You don't need a taxi, we bought a car this morning. It's not far to the boat,' he said, marching off.

'The boat, what boat?' said Tom following with Danny as Hank and Lance moved towards a rusty, beaten-up estate car.

The door creaked loudly as Hank pulled it open. Its red paint had faded so much you could barely tell where the paint stopped and the rust started.

'Fuck me, no expense spared. If the boat's anything

like the car, I doubt any of us will survive the mission,' said Danny managing a chuckle.

'Gotta blend in with the locals,' Hank laughed, grinding it into gear and driving off with a puff of diesel smoke hanging in the air behind them.

On their drive through Freeport, Danny found himself warming to Hank and Lance. He found out they were Delta Force boys and part of the team who disobeyed General Buchanan's orders and risked being shot getting the information to the president.

'Heads up, FirstCaribbean International Bank coming up on the right,' said Hank slowing down so they could get a good look.

The building looked more like a three-storey hotel to Danny than a bank. With a large car park out front, the building was painted yellow, which seemed to be the colour of choice in Freeport. It had a pitched, overhanging roof held up with four huge imposing white pillars. Very American colonial influence.

'It's big, got to be thirty or more people working in there,' said Danny winding the window down to get some air in the hot car.

'Yep, and I hope to hell one of them's called Mr Pozo,' said Lance.

As the car moved down Sea Horses Road, they turned into Port Lucaya Marina and parked up. Danny and Tom followed Hank and Lance as they walked along a wooden jetty towards a small boat moored next to a forty-foot millionaire's yacht. Danny and Tom stopped by the little boat ready to hop on board, to their surprised Hank and Lance continued walking.

'Not that one, buddy,' said Hank hopping onto the swim-up deck before climbing the steps to the main deck.

'I take it back, where the hell did you get this?' said Danny hopping across to follow them.

'Courtesy of the DEA and a busted drug smuggler. We sailed it over from Fort Lauderdale last night,' said Hank moving over to a lock box under one of the seats. He unlocked it and flipped it open.

'One good thing about coming by sea, we could bring a few essentials with us,' said Hank, pulling two heavy flight cases out and popping them on the seat. Flicking the catches, he opened them to show four Glock 17 handguns, silencers, and a set of Ontario MK3 combat knives in one case, and ultra-lightweight stab and bulletproof tactical vests with ammunition clips in the other case.

'It's not much, but it's better than nothing,' he said smiling.

'Not bad for a Yank,' said Danny, smiling back.

'I'll take that,' replied Hank.

'Look, it's too late to do much today, the bank will be shutting soon. Let's grab some grub and beers and figure out how we're going to tackle the bank and find Mr Pozo.'

CHAPTER 63

wo miles away from the marina a taxi pulled up to large colonial mansion on Gunport Boulevard. Its occupant pulled a small remote out of his suit pocket and pressed the button. The double electric gates swung open allowing the taxi to enter and head down a long palm tree lined drive towards the mansion. It rolled round the turning circle, stopping outside the steps to its imposing façade. The driver got out and scooted round to the boot of the taxi. He heaved two large suitcases out and wheeled them round to the passenger who stood waiting at the base of the white-painted steps that lead to large, solid front doors.

Yulan peeled off a fifty from a fat roll of dollars, waving the driver on his way when he attempted to provide change. The driver eagerly accepted the huge tip for an eight dollar fare and gave Yulan a business card before leaving. The Chinaman watched him as he went up the drive, stopping to let the automatic gates open before disappearing out of view behind the big wall that surrounded the property.

Picking the two heavy suitcases up with ease the Chinaman carried them up the steps. Unlocking the door he moved inside, leaving the cases on the shiny, white marble floor near the sweeping staircase that wound its circular way up to the bedrooms. Pushing a heavy door off the hall open, he entered a plush, panelled study and turned on the powerful computer. Yulan closed the sound-proofed door while it booted up. The panelling on the walls hid additional soundproofing and electronic equip-ment to stop any listening devices or camera equipment from transmitting outside the room. Taking a seat he waited as a secure satellite link loaded, its connection bar ticking cross the screen. When it reached 100% the chair-man's face appeared from his boardroom in Texas.

'I have arrived,' Yulan stated.

'So I see. You had no problem getting the cases through the airport?'

'No, our contact moved them through as usual.'

'Good. Take them to Pozo tomorrow, he knows what to do with them,' said the chairman, already disengaged from the conversation.

'Yes, fath—' Yulan started to say, his words cut short as the chairman terminated the call. He stood staring at the disconnected message on the screen, the faintest sign of sadness and the need for a father's love breaking through his usual emotionless mask. He buried the emotion in a flash and left the room. Grabbing the suitcases he carried them to the dining room and placed them on the banquet-sized table. Entering the combinations, he clicked the locks and opened them. He took a pair of ancient bagh nakh daggers off the top of one of the cases, placing the evil-looking weapons on the table. Their sharpened and polished S-shaped blades glinted in the sunlight from the window. The unusual handles had two loops that slid over

233

the index and little fingers. They had four razor-sharp blades like a tiger's claw running along the handle between the loops. When held, the claws protruded between the knuckles, with the curved blade sticking forward. The two weapons could inflict incredible damage as they stabbed and ripped their victim to pieces.

He turned back to the cases and took one of the banded piles of money off the top. After flicking through the wad of untraceable hundred-dollar bills, he put it back in its three-million-dollar pile which was duplicated in the other case. He closed the lids on the money destined to fund and bribe the reformed Board back into power. Yulan had done this trip many times. He would deposit it with Pozo at FirstCaribbean International Bank. From there, Pozo would earn his monthly payments by distributing the untraceable funds wherever the chairman instructed it to go.

Leaving the cases, Yulan went up the sweeping staircase and walked along the hall of his mother's family home to his bedroom. He changed into shorts and a sports vest while looking out of the window. The white sands and turquoise Caribbean Sea looked back at him from beyond the wall at the back of the mansion. Moving back downstairs, Yulan went out the back and walked around the swimming pool to a single-storey building at the rear of the garden. He entered the large gym with benches and racks of weights in one corner and running machine, cycles and cross-trainers in the other. The rest of the space was taken up with punch bags, pads and an old wing chun wooden training dummy. The end wall of the gym was covered with ancient weaponry, swords, spears, nunchaku, and an array of daggers. Yulan stretched and flexed, loosening up before moving to the wooden training dummy. He started slowly with rhythmic, practiced movements. The kung fu moves got steadily faster and harder, the thump of flesh on wood drumming out an ever-increasing beat as sweat poured off his face. He finished with a kick off the post that threw him into a backward somersault. He landed solidly on his feet, breathing heavily and glistening with sweat.

CHAPTER 64

anny rolled over in bed, the silk sheets feeling cool to the touch. He opened his eyes to see Kate's deep blue eyes looking into his, her long blonde hair falling over her bare shoulders. She smiled, displaying a mouth full of perfect white teeth, and said something. The words were soft and seductive, but he couldn't make out what they were. Sliding her arms around him she drew herself in, kissing him passionately. He closed his eyes, drinking in the smell of her perfume. When he opened them the image had disappeared. He was alone, awake and hollow. Rubbing his eyes before they formed a tear, Danny shook his head and leaped out of bed.

All up and dressed the four men wandered around the marina. Finding a table at a welcoming, sky-blue-painted café called Zorba's Café & Pastries, they ordered coffee and a selection of pastries. Falling back into barracks banter, the beer and jet lag of the night before soon cleared from Danny's head. He enjoyed the instant bond of comrades-in-arms, with the eat when you can, sleep when you can and fight when you have to mentality. With breakfast done, they creaked the car doors open and got in the rusty heap. Ignoring the puff of black smoke from its exhaust, they drove the couple of miles through Freeport, pulling into and parking in the far corner of FirstCaribbean International Bank's car park.

'Nothing for it, we'll have to go in and wing it,' said Danny.

'I'll come with you. You two hang back here, ok?' said Hank. Lance and Tom nodded their agreement.

'Right, here we go,' said Danny shaking his head at the car door as its dry hinges creaked loudly open. 'How much did you pay for this piece of shit?'

'Two hundred bucks. Government cutbacks, my friend,' said Hank with a chuckle.

They walked with relaxed confidence, the way any normal customer of the bank would. When they reached the doors, Hank pretended to have a call. He chatted to himself on the phone while Danny stood beside him, checking out the bank's foyer. Spying a pretty young black woman on reception, Danny wandered over with a wide smile and leaned on the desk.

'Good morning, sir. How can I help you?' she said with a sunny smile.

'Hi. A friend of mine opened an overseas account here last month and recommended I do the same. I think he saw a Mr Pozo. Would it be possible to make an appointment with him?'

'Mr Pozo? Erm, there's no Mr Pozo here. I wonder if he meant Mr Poltzman?'

'That does sound familiar, Sofia,' said Danny reading her name tag as he tried to look thoughtful.

'Well, that's Mr Poltzman in the corner. He's with a

client at the moment. If you'd like to wait, I'll see if he can see you when he's finished.'

Danny followed the direction of Sofia's glance, spotting a middle-aged black guy with short hair, little round glasses and a neatly trimmed beard. His client was sitting with his back to Danny. There was something familiar about the shape of his body in his cream cotton suit and his short jet-black hair. A few moments later the client turned his head slightly, showing a side profile as he talked to Poltzman. Recognition hit Danny like a punch to the chest.

'That's ok, Sofia,' Danny said composing himself. 'I haven't got the time now. I'll pop back later and make an appointment,' he said backing away from the desk, keeping his focus on the corner.

'Ok, sir. Have a nice day.'

'Er, thanks, you too, Sofia.'

Stepping out into the sunshine, Danny moved swiftly to the side of the door, grabbing Hank as he went.

'He's in there—the fucking Chinaman. Sitting with Pozo, or Poltzman as they know him,' said Danny shaking with rage, fighting the urge to fly at the Chinaman and snap his neck.

'Come on, let's back it up to the car.'

Reluctantly Danny nodded and they retreated to the corner of the car park and got in the car.

'The only two the Chinaman doesn't know are me and Lance. We'll follow him when he leaves and see where he goes. You two stay here and watch the bank. If Pozo leaves, you follow him, ok?' said Hank taking charge.

Danny wanted to argue but he knew Hank's plan made sense so he reluctantly agreed.

Checking their guns, Hank and Lance slid them in the belts of their jeans, covering them with their colourful Caribbean shirts. Danny watched them go. He punched the dashboard violently to release some anger, forcing the glove box to pop open.

'I know, mate. Be patient, your time will come. He'll pay.'

Danny sat back, his face hard as stone and his eyes burning as he watched Hank take position on a bench. He sat casually looking at his phone while Lance went to the other side of the bank's entrance door. Pulling a newspaper out of the bin, Lance sat pretending to read. Danny's phone rang with Hank's number.

'You ok with this, Danny?'

'Yeah, it's ok. I'm good.'

'Don't worry, I get it, he killed you girlfriend. When the time comes, he's yours, ok?' Hank said, looking straight at Danny from the bench.

'Heads up, the Chinaman's leaving the bank now,' said Danny, cutting him short.

'Roger that.'

Danny watched as the Chinaman walked on the pavement passing behind Hank. Lance got up from the far side and followed the Chinaman, keeping a steady twenty yards back. When Lance had gone past, Hank got up and fell into line ten yards behind him. A little further on Lance stopped to browse a shop window, letting Hank walk past to take the lead. Back in the car, Danny watched them like a hawk, his eyes locked on until all three of them disappeared from view. He looked at his watch. Nearly twelve.

Let's see if Pozo goes for lunch.

CHAPTER 65

The Chinaman's head never moved as Hank followed him. He maintained the same pace with his head forward as he passed a Burger King drive through, continuing on towards a complex of shops and restaurants. The internal clock in Hank's head ticked two minutes. He went down on one knee and pretended to tie a shoelace. Lance walked past him without looking his way, the internal clock in his head resetting as he took point. Crossing the street, the Chinaman walked around Bazzar Road before turning into the shopping complex. Lance stopped short on the corner of a shop by the entrance of the walkway to the bars and restaurants. Hank joined him and took a quick look down the walkway. The Chinaman was still walking with his back to them, his head forward. Hank took the lead, picking up the pace to bring himself twenty yards behind his target. Lance followed a uniform ten yards behind Hank. Staggered, they both watched the Chinaman turn out of sight where the walkway opened out into a square lined with cafés and shops and bars. Hank ran up to the corner with Lance tucking in behind him. He looked around to see a narrow alley leading out of the complex to the road, some thirty metres further along. The Chinaman was nowhere in sight.

'Shit,' grunted Hank breaking into a run.

'Where'd he go?' said Lance following.

'There's no way he could have run that in the time he was out of sight,' panted Hank reaching the end of the alleyway.

He glanced left and right and back behind him to the complex. No sign of the Chinaman. He'd disappeared like a ghost. They turned right and headed towards the back of the complex in the hope of spotting him again.

Yulan knew the minute he left the bank that he was being followed. The why and by who he didn't know. If he had to guess, he reckoned American military. Short buzz-cut hair, at attention posture while pretending to relax on the bench. Add a Californian tan and good teeth and you had U.S. military—Marine perhaps, or maybe Navy SEAL. Definitely special ops. He clocked Lance taking the lead in the reflection off a station wagon window. Continuing straight ahead he went past his parked Chrysler Exodus from the mansion, and headed for a small complex of bars, shops and restaurants off Bazzar Road. Another reflection. With no more than an eye movement the Chinaman noted Hank changing up to lead. Uniformed, regimented, a change every two minutes, the lead never getting any closer than twenty yards. He turned down the walkway into the complex, never changing his pace. *Twenty yards. He had about five seconds to move.*

Taking a hard right where the walkway opened out into a square, the Chinaman exploded into a run, heading for the narrow alley that ran out of the side of the complex. Counting the seconds off in his head, he leaped off a table and grabbed the railing of the balcony above. In one swift move he pulled himself level with the first-floor balcony and kicked backwards, somersaulting across the alley. As the second-count in his head hit five, he landed out of sight on the flat roof opposite. On the count of six he heard Hank's footsteps turn the corner before stopping.

'Shit.'

A second set of footsteps rounded the corner.

'Where'd he go?'

Two sets of footsteps ran to the end of the alley.

Peering over the edge of the flat roof, he saw Hank and Lance pause at the end of the alley before turning left towards the back of the complex. Nimbly dropping to the ground, the Chinaman straightened his jacket, leaving the complex the same way he came in. He kept an eye out for his tail as he doubled-back to his car. After a final check to make sure no one else was following him, he drove off heading for the mansion on Gunport Boulevard.

CHAPTER 66

'T he Yanks are back,' said Tom, sweating in the passenger seat of the old heap.

'Shit, I should have shot the fucker while I had a chance,' said Danny grimly.

'Yeah, outside a bank in The Bahamas, that would have been clever. You'd have been locked up in some shit pit prison for the next thirty years,' said Tom, stating the obvious to a brooding Danny.

'Mmm,' he grumbled back.

Hank and Lance approached looking fed up. They creaked the doors open and climbed in the back of the car.

'Don't ask,' said Hank.

'The bastard just vanished into thin air,' said Lance shrugging.

Poltzman didn't leave the building for lunch. Not wanting to risk losing two leads in one day by returning when the bank shut, they spent the afternoon camped out in the baking car watching the entrance doors. If there was one thing being in special ops taught you, it was how to wait. Several sweaty hours later the bank closed and staff started to filter out the door.

'That's him,' said Danny pointing Poltzman out to the rest of them.

'Where's he going? Car or on foot?' said Tom more to himself than anyone else.

Danny watched with one hand on the door handle ready to get out and follow if he continued on foot. Seeing him head for a red Golf, Hank started the engine and waited for Pozo to reverse out and drive past behind them. Backing out of the parking space, Hank turned onto the main road and followed the Golf at a safe distance. They didn't have to follow for long; Pozo turned onto Sea Horse Road and headed in the same direction as the marina. He took a right before it and turned down Westminster Drive into a residential area full of medium-sized single-storey homes. Dropping back, Hank gave Pozo more space as he drove slowly through the houses. The Golf pulled onto a drive and Pozo climbed out, relaxed and unaware of his tail. Hank drove a little further down the street as Danny turned and watched out the rear window.

'He's got his keys out. Yep, he's unlocking the door, so's there's probably no one else at home,' Danny said.

'How do you want to handle this?' said Hank.

Danny looked across at Hank, his face as dark as his mood after a long, disappointing day.

'Hard and heavy. Follow my lead,' he said pushing the door open with its familiar creak.

Danny walked up to the front door while the other three stayed out of sight by the Golf. With one hand behind him on the butt of his Glock 17, Danny pressed the doorbell and waited. He watched the distorted figure of Pozo approaching through the frosted pane of glass in the door. As soon as the lock clicked open and the door started to move, Danny fixed his best passive, smiley salesman face.

'Good afternoon, Mr Poltzman. Are we alone in the house today?'

'Er, what? Yes I... Sorry, who are you?' said Pozo, confused by Danny's familiarity and his friendly manner.

'Your worst fucking nightmare, pal,' Danny said, his face turning dark as he whipped his gun up under Pozo's chin, forcing him back inside. Hank and Lance followed Danny while Tom took a quick look around the quiet neighbourhood. With no one in sight, he entered and closed the door behind him.

Pushing Pozo backwards into the kitchen, Danny shoved him down into a chair, pistol-whipping him hard on the side of the temple. Through his SAS training he knew that instilling fear and dominance at first contact was paramount to extracting information quickly.

Terrified, Pozo put his hands over his painful head to stop Danny hitting him again.

'Please don't. Take anything. Just don't hurt me,' he cried out, his voice shaking.

Grabbing him by the throat, Danny lifted his head so he could see him and the three menacing men standing either side.

'One wrong answer—just one—and I put a bullet through your brain. Do you understand?'

Pozo nodded, his eyes desperately trying to avoid Danny's cold stare.

'Who is the chairman?' he said releasing his throat and placing the barrel of his gun on Pozo's forehead.

A new, more intense expression of fear spread across Pozo's face at the mention of the chairman.

'I don't know, I don't, honestly. He sends his man

down or he sends email instructions. I don't know anything about him,' he said, tears trickling down his cheek.

'We saw the Chinaman leave the bank this morning. Where is he?' Danny growled, his face inches away from Pozo's.

'Y-y-you saw the Chinaman. Oh no, oh God, I'm dead. He'll think I set him up, you've given me a death sentence.'

Pozo was crying now, a trail of snot coming out of his nose as he shook with fear.

'You better tell us where he is so we can take care of him then,' shouted Danny, his patience starting to wear thin.

'What are you going to do to me if I tell you?'

'I don't care about you, tell us where he is and we'll be on our way. Don't tell me and I'll kill you. Slowly and painfully,' Danny said, staring at him with the eyes of a killer.

'He stays at the Cooper's Mansion on Gunport Boulevard, he'll be there until tomorrow lunchtime. He checks the cash deposits have been distributed correctly in the morning, then leaves my commission in a briefcase in an airport locker on his way out.'

Danny stood back, leaving Pozo looking nervously between the four men. He relaxed ever so slightly, grasping the new-found hope that he might actually get out of this alive. With speed and power too fast for Pozo's shell-shocked brain to comprehend, Danny hit him with a massive blow on the side of Pozo's head. He flew off the chair like a ragdoll, thumping to the floor out cold.

'Tie him up,' said Danny tucking his gun into the back of his jeans. 'Let's go get the Chinaman,' he added heading for the front door.

CHAPTER 67

The road outside Pozo's was as quiet when they left as it was when they'd arrived. Danny was driving now and the pre-mission buzz charged the air.

'Boat first, we need to kit up,' said Danny to everyone's agreement.

The sun was setting as they boarded the seized millionaire's yacht. It cast its warm orange glow across the water before being swallowed by the horizon. They disappeared below deck, appearing minutes later in the darkest jeans and tops they could find. Hank dragged the equipment cases out onto the deck and opened them. He threw a tactical vest out to each man before putting the last one on himself, securing it into place with the velcro straps. They all took an Ontario MK3 combat knife and fitted it to the vest. Reaching into the other case Hank passed the silencers around. Danny grabbed one and screwed it to the end of his Glock. Finally, they took a spare magazine each, sliding them into the pocket on their vest. There was a final volley of clicking as they cleared their guns, checked the magazines and slid them back in and chambered a round.

'You all ready?' Danny said to the four men standing in front of him. 'We'll check the place out first and form a plan off-the-cuff, ok? Remember, this guy is dangerous. Even though I want to rip his heart out, we need to try to take him alive. He's the only one who can lead us to the chairman.'

They waited half an hour until full darkness descended on the marina. Checking no one was around they scooted to the car and headed for Gunport Boulevard and Cooper's Mansion. It didn't take long to cross the small town and find the boulevard. They followed it down to a sharp bend that took the road along the front of the shore-line properties. Cooper's Mansion wasn't hard to find with its high wall and solid gates. The name Cooper's Mansion was carved into a rectangle of masonry set into the wall by the heavy gates. They drove on without stopping and parked up on a slip road to the beach two properties down.

'Front's a no go. The house is too far back and there's no cover once you're over the wall. Let's check out the access off the beach,' Danny said, trying to open the door with minimal creaking.

'Where'd you get this fucking car?' whispered Tom, grinning.

They waited a while for their eyes to acclimatise to the dark, the coral sands and Caribbean Sea getting clearer as their pupils opened up to let more light in. Danny signalled to move out. They headed down the property line in single file until they were behind the wall of Cooper's Mansion. Splitting, they moved either side of a locked gate used for beach access. Tom crouched down with his back to the wall, cupping his hands to give Danny a leg up. Lance did the same on the other side of the gate, hoisting Hank up to see over the wall. The rear garden looked picturesque with dim lights along decorative paths that led up to an illuminated swimming pool by the rear of the mansion. There were some lights on in the main building but neither the Chinaman nor anyone else was in sight. Hank and Danny slid down to the ground and came close.

'Ok, can you pick the gate lock, Tom?'

'No problem,' said Tom, sliding his pick sticks out of the vest pocket.

'Once we're through, Lance, Hank you go left. Tom and I will go right. When we get into the house, we'll do a four-man sweep, quick and quiet. Hand signals only. If you have to shoot, shoot to wound; we'll take him with us.'

'Got it.'

'Roger that.'

Tom dropped to a knee and worked on the gate lock by touch, dropping the lock pins into position one by one.

CHAPTER 68

Yulan sat in the panelled study watching the familiar secure satellite link load in the middle of the three screens. It reached 100% and rang quietly as it waited for the recipient to answer. After thirty seconds, the chairman's face filled the screen.

'What is it?'

'When I left the bank I was followed by two Americans,' he said without undue concern.

'Mmm, did they tail you from the house or airport?' said the chairman, his voice full of annoyance but not with concern for his son.

'No, Father, I was not followed there. I believe they were there for Pozo. My being there was a matter of coincidence.'

'It is of no importance. Mr Poltzman doesn't know your true identity and the cash is untraceable. Terminate him before you leave, we will use Mr Suarez in the Cayman Islands for our future transactions—'

The screen to the left flicked into life as the chairman talked. A red box labelled Beach Gate flashed its protest.

Yulan tapped the keyboard to bring up the cameras located around the mansion. Greyscale pictures filled screens from the night sight cameras to the rear. Shadowy figures moved swiftly along each side of the rear garden towards the back of the house. Strong, decisive movements, trained, military.

'What is it, Yulan?' said the chairman impatiently.

Yulan removed his jacket and tie, placing them neatly over the back of a chair, his eyes never leaving the image of the men as they reached the back of the house.

'Excuse me, Father, I have company. I will be back shortly,' he said, hooking the bagh nakh daggers from the table over his fingers. He secured them in his grip, the razor-sharp tiger's claws visible between his fingers, and the glinting S-shaped blade sticking up from his thumbs. The screen beside him displayed the alarm as they breached the rear patio doors. From two thousand miles away the chairman watched as Yulan disappeared from his screen like a magician's trick. One minute he was there, the next he was gone.

CHAPTER 69

The pins in the patio door lock clicked inaudibly into line as Tom picked the lock. Standing up, he gave Danny a grin and pushed the glass door open. Danny swept in to one side with his gun up, covering the door on the far side of the room. Hank and Lance moved in front. In a well-rehearsed formation they crossed the room, taking up position either side of the door. Tom closed the back door and covered the rear. With his hand outstretched, Hank turned the handle and eased the door open. From further back, Danny checked it was clear while covering the space with his gun. He signalled for them to go forward. Hank and Lance moved through into the kitchen, separated and covered while Danny and Tom came in to join them.

The kitchen was large with a marble-topped island in the middle. A set of open double doors lay on the far side leading to a grand dining room. A door lay in the far corner. Danny guessed it led to the hallway and would be the direction to take for the rest of the sweep. Waving them forward, Lance took point and headed for the door.

Halfway there the house plunged into darkness. The four of them instinctively tightened formation. Hank and Lance covered the kitchen while Danny and Tom turned and covered the room they'd entered.

'Ok, the element of surprise has gone. Let's do this by the book. Full sweep, fast and hard,' said Danny, his eyes acclimatising to the dark details of the room slowly sharpening in the moonlight.

As Lance moved across the huge kitchen towards the door, Danny's senses tingled and the hairs on the back of his neck raised. There was a sense of movement across the room, like smoke swirling, fast and soundless. The Chinaman appeared in front of Lance, ripping deep grooves across the back of his gun hand with the dagger's claws, forcing him to drop the gun. Before it hit the ground, the Chinaman stabbed furiously at Lance's middle. Realising he was wearing a vest he ducked and slashed outwards across Lance's thigh with the claws. Spinning low out of sight behind the kitchen units, the Chinaman was gone before Lance hit the floor. Hank and Danny fired short blasts of metallic pings from their silenced Glocks as Lance cried out in pain. Cups, pans and tiles exploded off the wall in little ceramic chips. Danny covered the kitchen as the dust settled, while Hank and Tom moved in to grab Lance's hands and drag him out of the room.

'Tom, take him outside, try to stop the bleeding,' shouted Danny from the kitchen.

'Here, rip these up and tie them round his leg,' said Hank, passing some pool towels off the shelf.

Throwing them over his shoulder, Tom hoisted Lance upright and with his arm round him, helped him outside. Danny looked at Hank while sliding a full magazine into his gun. He held it in one hand and slid the combat knife out of its sheath with the other. Hank gave a wry smile, sliding a clip into his gun and pulling his knife out to match Danny.

'Let's get this fucker,' he said.

Nodding, Danny moved back into the kitchen taking care not to slip on the blood on the floor. He signalled Hank to go round the other side of the island in the centre of the kitchen. At the far end of the room the door to the hallway was now open. Danny wasn't buying it. No way the Chinaman ran off. He was close, waiting to attack. He looked across at Hank, who pointed at the open door to follow. Danny shook his head and pointed towards the dining room. Hank slid the knife back in its sheath and pulled out his mobile. He held it above his gun, nodded towards Danny and moved towards the dining room. Danny understood the intention and followed, his gun and focus in sync as he moved.

'One, two, three,' whispered Hank, hitting the light on the phone on three. Apart from the large banquet table and sixteen chairs that surrounded it, the room was empty.

Something wasn't right. Danny could feel it. Hank looked across at him.

'He must have gone through the other door,' whispered Hank turning to go for the hallway. Danny turned to go with him and realised what was bothering him.

'Hank, MOVE!' Danny shouted as the Chinaman powered the dining room door from behind. The door slammed into Hank's back with such force it sent him sliding across the kitchen floor on his front. In a flash of spinning motion, the Chinaman kicked Danny's gun away —he'd pulled the trigger but the bullet went wide, thudding its way through the door into the wall behind. The gun clattered along, disappearing somewhere under the table.

The Chinaman was still moving, his dagger glinting its way towards Danny's neck. On instinct Danny hooked his knife under the tiger's claws protruding through the Chinaman's knuckles. Twisting the blade, Danny swung his knee hard into the Chinaman's side, sending him flying into the chairs around the table. One of his antique knives slid out of sight.

The Chinaman was upright in a gravity-defying push off the floor. He hooked a chair with his foot and launched it like a penalty kick. It flew past Danny and connected with Hank's face as he was lining up a shot from the kitchen. The Chinaman and Danny stood facing each other, silhouettes in the gloom, each crouched slightly, each with a knife extended in one hand and an open palm on the other. Waiting. The Chinaman broke first, his arms and legs moving in a blur. Danny concentrated on the blade, blocking it knife-on-knife while his body got battered with kicks and punches. His eyes following every movement, he finally got an opening and powered a left hook into the Chinaman's face, feeling the cartilage give way. The Chinaman staggered back, a stunned look crossing his face as blood poured out of his nose. It was replaced a second later with fury. He spat the blood out of his mouth and charged at Danny. Bracing himself for contact, Danny recoiled as the Chinaman flew backwards to the sound of metallic pings. He crumpled to the floor under the table with a low moan. Looking back, Danny saw Tom standing in the kitchen, smoke drifting from his silencer.

CHAPTER 70

Y ou kill him?' said Danny.

'Nah, two in the leg, one in the shoulder,' said Tom still looking down the sights of his gun. Hank got up beside him wiping blood out of his eyes from a gash on his forehead.

'Find the fuse board, Tom. Get some bloody lights on, mate,' said Danny, trying to see the Chinaman under the table.

'Roger that,' Tom replied heading to the hallway while Hank covered the dining room.

No one moved until the house burst into painful bright light. As the stars cleared from their eyes, they saw dining room was empty. Hank and Danny followed a trail of blood from under the table to a door at the far end of the dining room. Tom joined them as they moved in formation down the hall. The blood disappeared through a door. They swept in on a count of three and found themselves in a study. The Chinaman was slumped in the office chair bleeding heavily as he leaned in and mumbled something at the computer screen.

'You disappointment me, boy,' came the chairman's voice from the speakers.

He leaned back in the chair looking at Tom, Hank, and Danny with hateful eyes as he gritted his teeth through the pain. He was in no fit state to fight, with blood flowing down his arm as it hung down unable to move with the bullet to the shoulder. He was losing a lot of blood from his leg and had taken his tie from the back of the chair and tied it around his thigh to stem the flow. Tom left Hank with his gun trained on the Chinaman and went to check on Lance outside. Danny moved into the room far enough to see the screen and found himself looking the chairman square in the face.

'Daniel Pearson, you are one persistent bastard.'

'I'm coming for you,' Danny growled back at him.

'Son, you've got nothing. You couldn't even give me a parking ticket.'

Danny squeezed the bullet wound in the Chinaman's shoulder, causing a grimace across his usually expressionless face. He leaned in towards the screen. 'He'll talk, they always do,' he said.

The chairman sat back in his boardroom chair and smiled. 'You have no idea who you're dealing with, boy. Goodbye, Mr Pearson.'

The chairman leaned forward and tapped his keyboard. The screen in the centre went blank before all three lit up with a chain sequence of boxes turning red one after another.

Armed One.

Armed Two.

Armed Three.

'Hank, get out. Get out NOW!' Danny shouted, moving for the door.

'What about him?' Hank said running with him down the corridor.

'No time. Go, go.'

They hurtled down the corridor, a high-pitched whistle coming from behind the walls as detonators charged, pushed them on harder. Passing through the dining room Hank bumped into the kitchen units as he skidded in the blood on the marble floor. Danny grabbed the collar of his tactical vest as he passed, yanking Hank along with him. They entered the far room and got within an arm's length away from the patio doors when charges blew. The boom blew the glass out in front of them first, followed by the blast wave a fraction of a second later. It slammed them in the back, picking them up and catapulting them into the pool. They plunged under the water while a huge fireball rolled across the water's surface above them. Glass, bricks, and debris plonked into the water all around them as the fireball disintegrated. Danny broke the surface gasping for air with Hank close behind. They dragged themselves out and turned to see the mansion reduced to a wrecked inferno.

'Fuck, where's Tom and Lance?' said Danny, spinning around to find them.

'They're over there, by the gate to the beach,' said Hank barely hearing him past the ringing in his ears.

'Let's get fuck out of here,' Danny said dripping his way down the garden.

They picked Lance up under the armpits and moved as fast as they could along the beach to the car. They eased Lance into the passenger seat, a blood-soaked beach towel tied tightly around his leg.

'Hold tight, mate, we'll soon get you out of here,' said Danny crunching the car into gear.

'I'm good. He cut deep but didn't hit an artery. Tom's

258

stopped the bleeding for now,' said Lance wincing through the pain.

Danny turned right onto Gunport Boulevard, taking them away from the collapsing fireball of the mansion glowing in the sky behind them. Twenty minutes later they pulled into the quiet marina. After waiting for a couple to disappear out of sight, they got Lance on to the yacht and cast off. Hank cruised out to open sea before gunning the powerful engines to the max, heading for Fort Lauderdale. As soon as they were in U.S. waters, Hank got on the radio and had a U.S. Navy helicopter fly out and airlift Lance to a military hospital on the mainland. The beautiful million-aire's yacht gurgled into Fort Lauderdale harbour in the early hours of the morning. Three U.S. Army Humvees sat on the quay waiting for them. Hank shut the engines down while Danny and Tom hopped onto the quay and tied the boat off.

'Sergeant,' Hank said, saluting the young officer.

'Sirs, General Parnell requests your attendance. If you will come with us there's a plane waiting to take you to Washington.'

'Thank you, Sergeant,' said Hank.

'Any chance of a shower first?' said Danny, smiling. They'd changed out of their wet clothes back in Grand Bahama, but Danny's face was still smoke-smudged and his unruly hair was sticking up, singed.

'Sorry, sir, there's no time. Please,' he said gesturing to the Humvee as a soldier opened the back door.

Shrugging, Danny slung his old army backpack on his shoulder and followed Hank and Tom to the vehicle.

CHAPTER 71

The chairman moved into his newly fitted out boardroom. He checked the powerful PCs inside their metal rack cabinet hidden behind an oak panel door. They had removed the last of the old computers, their hard drives wiped and destroyed. He looked at the wall of monitors at the far end of the room. With any incriminating evidence now gone it was time to rebuild.

It was a shame about Yulan, but at least that link back to him was now closed. They may know who he was but nobody could prove anything. If anyone came for him his lawyers would rip them to pieces. The chairman caught sight of the photo of his late wife with the three Chinese babies in her arms. Cold as he was he couldn't bring himself to look at her. He never loved the boys, not like she did. Sliding the drawer out he turned the picture face down and slid it shut, out of sight. Sitting back in his plush leather chair he tapped at the phone and called Lei. The phone rang for eight rings then diverted to the standard service provider's mailbox message. The chairman didn't leave a message, he just hung up, his face contorting in annoyance and frustration.

Where the hell is that useless boy?

His mobile pinged with a reminder snapping him out of his mood. He got up and left the boardroom, false pleasantries back on his face as he approached his secretary.

'Hold my calls, Sandy. It's a beautiful day. I'm off to teach Senator Matthews a lesson in golf.'

'Very good, sir, have a good game,' she said in a well-rehearsed sunny voice and pretend interest.

'Thank you, Sandy,' he said walking out of the office.

CHAPTER 72

The U.S. Air Force jet touched down at Anacostia-Bolling, Washington D.C. Three tired and dishevelled passengers walked down the steps to salutes and a waiting black Lincoln limousine. Hank and Tom saluted the officer back. Danny didn't, he just gave a nod, he was technically a civilian after all.

'Where are we going?' said Danny through the open glass divider between the driver and passenger compartments.

'I'm to take you to the Pentagon, sir,' the driver replied.

'The only place I want to go is bed,' grumbled Danny.

'You and me both,' said Tom, still brushing flakes of Lance's dried-up blood off his forearms.

The journey didn't take long and after the expected security checks the car drove up to the steps below the pillared entrance of the Pentagon. An officer from the armed escort team opened the car door. More mutual saluting and a courtesy nod from Danny entailed as they got out and followed the escort inside.

The size of the Pentagon with its layers, floors, and miles of shiny corridors was hard to comprehend. Reaching a set of heavy double doors, the armed guard either side saluted before opening them for the three to enter. Inside the meeting room, eight men around a large conference table stood to greet them. At the head of the table stood the President of the United States. Danny recognised General Parnell on his right and Deputy Chief of the FBI Patrick Fallen sitting further down the table.

'Gentlemen, it's a pleasure to have you with us. Master Sergeant Meadows, it's good to see you again. Mr Pearson and Mr Trent, I believe you know General Parnell and Deputy Chief Patrick Fallen. Please have a seat and I'll introduce you to the rest of the room.'

The president went round the table introducing foreign advisors and members of his security council. When he'd finished, Danny leaned on the table.

'Mr President, I'm not sure why you've gone to the trouble of bringing us all this way. Our trip to Grand Bahama was unsuccessful. Other than seeing his face, we didn't find any information leading to the identity of the chairman. He blew the mansion and the Chinaman up before we could interrogate him.'

'Don't be so hard on yourself, son. Mr Fallen, would you like to enlighten Mr Pearson on the new information in play?' said General Parnell.

'Certainly, General. Cooper's Mansion has been in the Cooper family for over a hundred years. When Stanley and Irene Cooper died they left the estate to Maria Cooper. When Maria Cooper married a Texan oil tycoon by the name of Buster Merridew, the fourth richest man on the planet, she moved to Texas and kept Cooper's Mansion as a holiday home. Maria and her parents had been avid environmentalists. She tirelessly campaigned against deforestation, pollution and global warming through fossil fuel emissions. So much so she convinced her husband to invest heavily in clean energy solutions across the globe,' said Fallen pausing to take a sip of water.

'Maria Cooper-Merridew couldn't have children so, desperate to be a mother, she adopted three children from China—triplets to be precise—Tan, Yulan and Lei. Tragically, she was diagnosed with cancer when they were young and died six months later. Grief-ridden, Buster couldn't bear to look at the boys and sent them away to board in the finest schools. When they were older they embraced their love of martial arts and went to study in China and Japan. Maria left Cooper's Mansion in trust for the boys when they turned 21. With a lack fatherly love, they took their mother's name of Cooper which is why we couldn't link them to the chairman or find their identities.'

'Sorry, did you say triplets? So there's another one out there?' interrupted Danny.

'No, according to records, Lei Cooper died in a boating accident when he was eighteen, his body was never found,' said Fallen finishing up.

'Right, so Buster Merridew is the chairman then. Can you prove it?' said Danny, stifling a yawn.

Fallen slid a photo of Buster Merridew in front of them.

'Is that him?' he said.

'Yep, can you prove it?' said Danny repeating the question.

'Not yet, but we have teams of agents on their way with federal warrants to arrest Buster Merridew and to seize all computers and paperwork from Merridew Oil.'

'So that's it then,' said Hank.

'That's it for you guys. We'll let the American justice system and the FBI take it from here,' said the president, standing. He walked round the table and extended his hand to Danny.

'I just wanted to shake you gentlemen by the hand and extend our thanks.' He shook their hands and called the officer from the door over.

'I've taken the liberty of booking suites for all of you at the Conrad Hotel. The bill is on Uncle Sam so enjoy yourselves. You've earned it. One of my aides will arrange first class flights for you and Mr Trent back to London tomorrow.'

Meeting over, the three of them were escorted back through the maze of shiny corridors and layers of security until they were out the doors and back in the waiting Lincoln limousine. Within the hour they were checked in like royalty to the five-star Conrad Hotel. Danny finally got his shower and a change of clothes. The hotel suite was the largest he'd ever seen, let alone stayed in. He met Hank and Tom in the restaurant. The three of them ordered generously on the president's tab. They sat oblivious to the frowns and comments from the well-to-do at their scruffy jeans and T-shirts. Danny's unruly hair was sticking up and singed, while Hank had a partly burnt-off buzz-cut and stitches across his forehead. They ate and drank and laughed, Danny keeping the thoughts of Kate at bay until he was alone in his suite later that night.

CHAPTER 73

Buster Merridew met Senator Matthews on the terrace of the clubhouse to the prestigious Whispering Pines Golf Club. The club caddies loaded their bags onto the back of the golf cart and drove them along the lush green grass to the first hole.

'Your turn to tee off, Gregory. Fancy a little wager?' said Buster marching ahead of the caddies as they fetched the golf bags.

'Don't mind if I do. One thousand dollars to the winner,' said the senator loud enough for the minimum wage caddies to hear.

'Done. Easiest money I ever made,' laughed Buster.

'Don't count your money just yet,' the senator replied. 'Three wood,' he said gruffly to the caddy.

He powered the golf ball cleanly down the fairway, landing 50 yards short of the green on the par three hole.

'Fighting talk. I like it,' said Buster, unzipping the pocket at the front of his golf bag and pulling a pair of leather golf gloves out. Their heads turned at the sound of sirens in the distance.

'What the hell it that?' Buster said pulling his glove on.

'Don't know, are the sirens really that necessary?'

'Mmm, I'll make a complaint to the cl— ouch!' Buster said as something sharp in the right golf glove pricked his skin.

He felt his fingers going numb as he pulled the glove off. By the time it hit the floor Buster couldn't move his arm.

'Gregory help m—' he started to say before his throat tightened.

The senator turned to look at him, his face dropping when he saw the panic on Buster's face as he dropped to his knees.

'Go and get help!' he shouted to the caddy over the sound of the sirens. He gently laid Buster on the grass while the caddy ran off towards the clubhouse.

Buster looked at the sky through eyes that he couldn't shut. Control left his diaphragm and he couldn't draw breath. The thump of his heart slowed and faded until it pumped no more. In his mind he was screaming, terrified at his imminent demise. He could see the senator over him, his mouth was moving but Buster couldn't hear him anymore. The image faded into black and Buster faded away with it.

———

A cavalcade of FBI vehicles screeched to a halt outside the clubhouse. Agents hurried into the foyer, much to the disgust of the club members. They showed badges and demanded the whereabouts of Buster Merridew. The shocked receptionist pointed them in the direction of the course. The caddy burst in out of breath before they could make a move. He was panicking and talking fast about Mr

Merridew collapsing. The agents rushed out as he led the way. The line of black suits running across the green course cast an odd image as they headed en masse toward the first hole.

Sitting in a plush leather chair in the exclusive clubhouse bar, Lei sipped iced tea while he watched the scene unfold. He felt an unaccustomed wave of happiness, his mouth curling into a rare smile as the neurotoxin from the Columbian golden frog ended his domineering father's life. He finished his tea, left a tip on the table and stood up, straightening his cream linen suit jacket. Sliding his sunglasses on he casually walked out of the building, past the onlooking FBI agents, to his car. While the agents were trying their hardest to resuscitate Buster Merridew at the first hole, the Chinaman drove steadily out of the car park heading for the freeway.

CHAPTER 74

Danny and Tom walked through arrivals at British Airways Terminal 5, Heathrow. Danny felt unusually refreshed after the journey. But then again, he didn't usually travel in the spacious luxury of first class, with champagne and a three-course meal of lobster tortelloni, Hertfordshire beef, and warm apricot sponge pudding. He'd eaten half of Tom's as well to fill himself up, which was ok as Tom was nursing a big hangover from the night before. They exited into warm sunshine and fresh English air. A familiar large black limousine parked in the pick-up bay spoiled the moment. The armed police—who usually move anyone on who stops for anything longer than a minute—gave the vehicle a wide berth. Its driver walked round to the passenger side and opened the door as they approached, gesturing for them to get in. Danny put his hand on the roof of the car and bent down to look in.

'Welcome back, Daniel. Do get in, there's a good chap,' said Howard, crutches by his side.

'You've lost the wheelchair then,' said Danny, climbing in with Tom behind him.

'Yes. Still a bit stiff but well on the mend.'

'What do you want, Howard?' said Danny, always skeptical of the government man.

'Nothing, dear boy, I'm here to extend the gratitude of the English government and the prime minister to the both of you. Our appreciation has been deposited in your usual accounts with an additional contribution from our friends across the pond.'

'This means we're done, you and me, the debt paid, finished,' said Danny, a fiery look in his eyes.

'That's a very fluid concept, Daniel, but yes we're finished. For now,' said Howard, his gaze holding its own against Danny's.

'Right, off you trot, you two, things to do and all that,' said Howard signalling for the driver to open the door.

They got back out and watched the limousine pull silently away into the distance.

'I swear, one day I'm going to kill that bastard myself,' said Danny, shaking his head.

'You'll have to get in line, mate,' said Tom with a chuckle. 'Come on, let's share a cab. My place isn't far from yours.'

CHAPTER 75

Three months after Buster Merridew's death, the FBI had closed the case on the board down. Not a scrap of hard evidence had been found at Buster's estate on the outskirts of Dallas or at Merridew Oil. A new company CEO had been appointed by the shareholders, and Buster's multi-billion-dollar estate had been passed on to an undisclosed beneficiary.

There was a buzz around the office as the new CEO of the company would be taking over today. At midday a limousine turned into the company headquarters and pulled up to its plush entrance. The chauffeur hopped out and quickly moved round to the passenger side. He opened the door and a young man in his mid-twenties stepped out. He straightened his tailored charcoal-grey suit jacket and walked into the building. After greeting the employees in reception, he made his way through the offices. He smiled and greeted everyone as he went. Eventually he got to his new office and the woman who would be his secretary.

'Good afternoon, Sandy. It's so good to see you again and I look forward to working with you,' he said.

'Good afternoon, Mr Cooper. I look forward to working with you too,' she replied with a shy smile.

'Is anyone in the boardroom? I have a few calls to make.'

'No, Mr Cooper. It's free.'

'Lei. Just call me Lei,' the Chinaman said with a smile.

He moved into the boardroom and sat in the big leather chair. Looking around, he slid open one of the drawers and stopped still at something inside. Carefully removing it, he placed the picture of his mother holding him and his baby brothers back into its rightful place on the cupboard to the side of the room. Tearing his gaze away he looked at the time on his Rolex Daytona watch. With a small smile on his face he tapped at the keyboard and watched the screens burst into life. The secure satellite connection bar moved up on each one before eight faces filled the screens.

'Welcome, gentlemen. Let us celebrate this truly monumental day. As the majority shareholders in Merridew Oil, we have full control and the freedom to use the considerable assets at our disposal for the good of our planet. As you know, it was my mother's dream to use the money my father made off the back of the oil industry to develop cheap green energy and sustainable ecological solutions to better the world. My father twisted that dream and turned it into a global power play. Gentlemen, with your help we are going honour my mother's legacy. We are going to give technology and cheap energy with clean drinking water to the third world countries, thanks to Cheng Haku's hydrogen energy plants now run by the late Cheng Haku's brother, Zahang Haku.'

'Thank you, Mr Chairman,' said Zahang nodding in respect.

'We are going to subsidise batteries' technology and

install free charging points across the globe for the electric car industry with the help of Mr Ian McClusky of ECB.'

'Thank you, Mr Chairman,' said Ian McClusky, smiling for the centre monitor.

'Not forgetting the enormous advances in wave power technology from our Dutch colleague, Malcolm Janssen from WaveGen.'

'Thank you, Mr Chairman,' said Malcolm Janssen.

'None of this would be possible if it weren't for the political negotiations and expertise from our ambassadors across the globe, Senator Gregory Matthews and our Russian emissary, Karl Lemitov.'

'Thank you, Mr Chairman,' they said in unison.

'And lastly, our new European delegate, Hanz Schiffer, and African diplomat, Nile Babona.'

'Thank you, Mr Chairman.'

'Now that you are all acquainted, I would like to reveal the new company name—after my late mother—Cooper's World Energy,' said the new chairman, finishing his speech.

Starting with Ian McClusky, the members of the board started to clap until they were all in rapturous applause.

CHAPTER 76

Things at Greenwood Security settled back into their normal routine. Danny sat in his office working out schedules and manpower for upcoming contracts. Paul had fully recovered and was in and out of meetings with clients and officials. Although physically ok, Danny still struggled with the emotional effects of the losses in his life: his wife and child killed by Nicholas Snipe, and Kate killed by the Chinaman. Both times he'd not been able to save them and now he carried two lots of guilt buried deep within him, burning, never forgotten. His phone rang, offering him a welcome distraction to his thoughts.

'Yep,' he answered.

'Daniel, old boy, I've got two hot blondes and reservations at Kanishka. Say hello, girls.'

'Hi, Danny,' came two giggling voices in unison.

'What the hell is Kanishka and who are the giggling twins, Scott?' said Danny. Scott always knew how to make him smile.

'Ahh, Kanishka is a very exclusive restaurant, you

caveman, Indian food. Amazing place, and the twins are Misha and Anouska. They're swimwear models from Lithuania. Need I say any more?' said Scott, obviously enjoying the moment.

'Go on then, what time are we going?'

'Right now, old man. We're in The London Cocktail Club on Great Portland Street. Shake a leg and get down here.'

'Come on, Danny, hurry up,' came the giggles in the background.

'Alright, alright, I'm coming,' said Danny, putting the phone down.

He got up and grabbed his jacket, popping his head into Paul's office on his way out. 'I'm heading off, Paul. I'll see you tomorrow.'

'Ok, going anywhere nice?'

'I'm going to save Scott from the Lithuanians,' shouted Danny walking out of the office.

———

The taxi drew up outside Danny's house sometime around 2:00 a.m. He got out to the protests of Misha and Anouska.

'Danny come back to Scott's. We have more drinks, more fun, ya,' they cried from either side of Scott grinning his head off.

'No, sorry, girls. I've got a busy day at work tomorrow,' Danny said, feeling a little too old for that much partying.

'Your loss, old boy. Driver, take me home,' laughed Scott rather worse for wear.

Danny watched them leave. He took a big breath of chilly London air and let himself into his house. Chucking his keys into a bowl in the hall, he hung his coat on the coat hook, kicked his shoes off and padded through to the kitchen. He opened the fridge and took a big swig of orange juice from the carton. Yawning as he put the juice back he headed up the stairs to bed. Just short of the top step his senses tingled. The hairs on the back of his neck stood up. He whipped his head round to see the bottom of the stairs. Nothing. Totally still. He listened to the sounds of the house as it hummed and ticked its usual homely sounds. Shaking it off, he went into the bedroom.

———

Yulan moved silently out of the shadows. The Chinaman stood at the bottom of the stairs listening. He cocked his head to one side and listened to the sounds of Danny moving around the bedroom. The other side of his head was hairless, burnt and scarred, his left ear burnt completely off leaving just a gristly hole in the red, still-healing skin. Minutes passed until he heard bedsprings flex and the bedside lamp clicking off. Reaching into his suit jacket he pulled out two silver daggers, ancient engravings etched along each blade. He waited another five minutes then moved up the stairs like a ghost, floating effortlessly without a sound as he ascended to the landing.

The Chinaman pushed the bedroom door open with an astonishing amount of control, so slowly the door couldn't creak, taking over a minute to open it far enough to enter. With his eyes accustomed to the dark he could see the outline of Danny in the bed. He made his way round beside his sleeping prey. A flicker of a revengeful smile crept across his face as he raised the daggers and plunged them in mid-torso.

The daggers slid much too fast into the soft shape in

the bed. In the same instant he felt the pressure from the cold barrel of a gun on the back of his head.

'You ain't that fucking good, this is for Kate,' whispered Danny.

Even with the Chinaman's lightning reflexes, he couldn't have got out of the way fast enough. With his face like granite and pupils large and cold in the darkness, Danny pulled the trigger and watched the front of the Chinaman's face explode over the bed.

CHAPTER 77

inutes after leaving a message at Oxford Financial Consultants for Howard, the phone rang back.

'Daniel, to what do I owe this unexpected pleasure?'

'I have a dead Chinaman in my bedroom,' said Danny gruffly.

'That's unfortunate for you, how did he die?' said Howard in a jovial tone.

'Bullet through the head,' said Danny, failing to see the humour.

'Tut, tut, tut, Daniel. An illegal firearm, a dead body. What a pickle. That's a thirty-year stretch,' said Howard enjoying the upper hand.

'Cut the crap, Howard.'

'It will mean you being in my debt again.'

'Just send a clean-up crew,' growled Danny, annoyed to be back in the government man's pocket.

'Take a walk, Daniel, or better still, get in a taxi and join Scott and his Lithuanian friends. Don't come back until dawn.'

The phone went dead before Danny could question Howard on how he knew where he'd had been all night.

He didn't call Scott. He just threw on his coat and left the house, walking off into the early morning gloom.

ABOUT THE AUTHOR

Stephen Taylor was born in 1968 in Walthamstow, London.

I've always had a love of action thriller books, Lee Child's Jack Reacher and Vince Flynn's Mitch Rapp and Tom Wood's Victor. I also love action movies, Die Hard, Daniel Craig's Bond and Jason Statham in The Transporter and don't get me started on Guy Richie's Lock Stock or Snatch. The harder and faster the action the better, with a bit of humour thrown in to move it along.

The Danny Pearson series can be read in any order. Fans of Lee Child's Jack Reacher or Vince Flynn's Mitch Rapp and Clive Cussler novels will find these books infinitely more fun. If you're expecting a Dan Brown or Ian Rankin you'll probably hate them.

Printed in the USA
CPSIA information can be obtained
at www.ICGtesting.com
CBHW011114270324
5938CB00023B/1713

9 781739 163624